CELEBRATE
THE
MORNING

Ella Thorp Ellis

CELEBRATE
THE
MORNING

Atheneum 1976 *New York*

FOR MOTHER

CELEBRATE
THE
MORNING

I

SOMETIMES, IN OUR PART OF CALIFORNIA, WE HAVE what we call a very late Indian summer; sandwiched between a black frost and a week's pelting rain, there may come a day as warm and blue as any in May. Only it is better. I don't know whether this is because it seldom lasts more than two or three days or because in the scattering leaves, the musky smell of steaming roofs and earth, there really is a chrysanthemum tang that incorporates spring pleasures but adds something else. Maybe I only feel this way because my birthday comes in November.

On such a day, the week before my fourteenth birthday, I was sauntering down the alley toward our house. The dirt was so warm I had taken off my

3

sandals, and I dug my toes into the pliant sand and twirled. I thought that in my peasant skirt and blouse, with my long dark hair flying, I must look like a gypsy and it gave me pleasure to think that the people who might see me wouldn't recognize me as a ballerina. They might stare, but they could not see me, not really.

Fermine, the elderly man who lived next door, was standing at his gate, I suppose scanning the sky for rain. He didn't like disorderly unseasonable weather. It made the fruit trees swell before their time so the blossoms would be nipped by the frost, which was surely coming. Fermine relied on natural disasters. He had been a farmer all his life and felt that each ear of corn he had ever harvested had been a victory over the armies of earth and sky and insects.

I knew he was there, but I had closed my eyes to feel only the delicious dizziness, and so it was that I twirled right into him, knocking us both off balance. He felt like a warm telephone pole, and he smelled like sweet hot chilies and the lavender soap he made himself.

"Umph. Stupid kid."

"Fermine, Fermine. Don't be grouchy. It's such a supremely glorious day, and you were just *there*—in the path of the dance. See?" I pirouetted before him, dislodging a horney toad, which scurried across the alley and disappeared under a pile of wood. My toes dug deeply and surely into the sand, my arms joined

4

in an arch over my head. I went up on my toes but the toad and the disapproving look on Fermine's face made me laugh, and I stumbled, sprawling face down in the alley, eating dirt.

"Stop that!" Fermine bellowed. "You are too old for such shamelessness, such showing your legs. You should be at home, helping your mother. If you were mine——"

"Preserve me from such a horrible fate," I said, dusting myself off. Fermine's face looked tired and thin under his great white beard. "I know, you're a vegetarian again? Oh, yes, you are. I can see it in your face. No wonder you're unbearable. It's just that you're hungry."

Fermine drew himself up, raised his chin, and stared me down. He wore old overalls and a straw hat, but when he stretched himself up furiously like that, I knew he was right about coming from a family who had once owned most of the county, having been given it by the King in Mexico. I never teased any more when he got like that. As I watched him, however, he did an unusual thing. He wiped his face with a handkerchief, passing it over the whole of his expression like a magician doing a rabbit trick and, when he was done, he was smiling. It was a sad smile, and I felt mean.

He took an old pair of garden clippers, carefully wrapped with electrician's tape, and snipped half a dozen late blooming Talisman roses from a vine running along the top of his fence. He wiped the clippers on his overalls and put them back in their usual pocket, and then he handed me the roses.

"Here. Mind you put them right in water."

"Roses from an admirer! Just like a real ballerina after a performance. I could kiss you." I reached for Fermine, but he ducked out of my grasp and disappeared behind his gate.

"Doesn't matter," he said.

"Fermine, you're blushing!"

My mother was sitting in an old webbed lounge chair in the back yard, pulling out white hairs. She sometimes did this when she sat out in the sun, and it always made me slightly sick to my stomach. In the first place she had long straight hair and the grey made her look dignified, like an Irish poet; and in the second place, pulling them out was lying about her age. It was even worse than tinting your hair to hide the grey, since it must hurt and might leave you bald eventually; but she would throw her hair down in front of her eyes and work for hours. Therefore, she didn't see me coming. I could have stood there until it got too dark to tell the white from the black.

"I just don't understand why you bother. You don't have any boyfriends, and you and Dad have been divorced for years," I said.

My mother parted the hair then and peered out at me but said nothing.

"Is Fermine a vegetarian again? I bumped into him, purely by accident, and he almost took my head off," I said, waving the roses under her nose.

She sniffed, smiled, and went back to her hair. She found an elusive strand of white, pulled, examined the hair at arm's length for a long moment, and then dropped it. She ran a comb quickly through her hair and tied it back with a white shoelace. "Ah, poor man. Poor, poor man," she said, finally.

Mom seemed to be thinking aloud rather than starting a conversation, so I dumped my books in the house, made us each a cheese sandwich and some iced coffee, and took them back outside. I watched her add three heaping teaspoons of sugar to her coffee. My mother lived on sugar, cinnamon rolls, Hershey's chocolate bars, and canned fruit cocktail. She was thinner than a Vogue model. I gained weight just watching her eat. Still thinking of something else, she had a sad smile when she looked at me.

"Hey, what's wrong with everybody? First Fermine and now you. You always say you wait all day for me to come home from school. Well, here I am."

"Beautiful as usual," she said absently.

"Has Fermine been over here?"

She nodded.

"He ask you to marry him again? I thought so. Dirty old man with his false teeth clacking away!" Fermine had once been the person I loved best, after

my mother, but everything about him physically nau-
seated me after he started pestering Mom to marry
him.

"April, don't. I only said he was too old for *me*, not
to marry. He *was* married once to a very beautiful
woman——"

"You never told me he was married!"

"Yes, she died in childbirth. They weren't always
so sanitary in those days——"

"Never mind, never mind, mother. Spare me the
gory details." Every year about this time my mother
would start talking about childbirth and wind up on
mine. She seemed to think I *liked* spending each and
every birthday hearing about her long labor, how I
weighed close to ten pounds, how the entire world expected me to be a hairy boy but instead I was a girl,
how she named me April because she yearned for daffodils, and on and on. It was an annual horror movie.

"Did the present from Dad come?" I asked, ignoring her hurt look.

"This morning. Special Delivery, no less. I had to
sign for it."

I ran into the house. The sun was still in my eyes,
so I was sifting through the darkness as well as a
week's dirty dishes and the usual welter of clothes
and wilting flowers and magazines covering every
available surface in our kitchen and studio-bedroom.
My father always sent a combined birthday-Christmas
present, and it was usually stupendous. The year be-

fore he'd sent a radio-phonograph, and the year before that, a bicycle. I think he felt guilty because
Mom never asked a cent in child support and that's
why I lucked out. But, as Mom said, why harass the
poor man when we got by just as well on welfare? I
have never happened to meet my father, who lives in
the East, but I get some idea of who he thinks *I* am by
what he sends every year.

That year I had no idea what to look for, how big
the package might be, or how it might be wrapped. I
only knew it came Special Delivery. Then, because
I'd begun looking on top of the book cases, I stumbled, hit the rocking chair, upset a full cup of coffee,
and landed just short of a large square box about the
size of a case of dog food.

"Oh, no, not this!" I groaned. It certainly didn't
look like the kind of box I wanted to spend a week
of my life worrying about. But there was Special Delivery stamped all over the place. Four dollars and
seventy-eight cents in stamps. Almost enough to buy
a sweater. Miss April Mitchell. As I said, I was named
April because I was born during a storm in November. I sat up and pulled the box onto my lap. It must
have weighed at least 25 pounds. Solid. Nothing
shook. All I needed was a set of encyclopedias, leather-
bound. Like a hole in the head. The box wasn't all
that heavy, actually, but it was no fur coat or anything else I could wear. Sometimes my father wrote
and told Mom. She wouldn't tell me on purpose, but

she had been known to slip.

"All right, I give up. What is it?" I yelled through the open door.

No answer. I got up stiffly, mopped at the coffee with a towel, and hobbled to the door. I ached, but nothing seemed to be broken. My mother was still sitting on the chaise lounge, staring into space. Not blinking. The wind had come up, and it whipped her hair over her face. She didn't notice and also seemed oblivious of the goosepimples on her bare arms. It was a cold wind, blowing the last leaves from the cherry tree, knocking bark and balls from the eucalyptus and sending them scattering across our yard and on into the vacant lot on the other side of the alley. The birds were jittery, and chattering the way they do before a storm. Then a rumble of thunder bounced across the gathering sky. Still my mother sat immobile, as if she were in dead calm, already in the eye of the coming storm, or yet in the sun of an hour before.

"Hey, come to. What's in the box from Dad, what is it?" I asked. I waited. She didn't even know I was there. In the alley a dog barked. Thor, meanest Doberman in the world. Somehow the bark released me from the silence, and I shook her by both arms and repeated the question. Slowly her eyes focused.

"What? The box? Present? Oh, yes, of course, *that* box. Tattle-tale-tit, his tongue shall be slit," she said, as she had for every birthday I could remember.

But she said it sing-song, like a Mother Goose rhyme, and she did not look at me.

"At least tell me if you know. That's not much when it's still a whole week 'till my birthday," I begged, lifting her under the arms and heading us both toward the house.

"A week? I wonder if a week breaks apart like an orange," she said.

"I'll never live through it," I said, easing my mother into the house and closing the door against new thunder.

2

THE THUNDER DID NOT BRING RAIN, AND FOR DAYS THE sky hung like a dull silver balloon. Any minute a pin might puncture that ominous globe and, when the rain came pouring out, winter would begin. Meanwhile, we waited.

Fermine worked in his garden and in his fields by the edge of town; staking, trenching, pruning, battening down his plants against the storm he felt coming. He was forever looking up at the sky, hoping to finish in time. When he had done everything a farmer could do and the weather still hovered, still waited, then he took down his mandolin and sat by his window, plucking at old Spanish tunes. He played loudly, off-key, and all day.

That mandolin was the last straw for my mother. The impending storm depressed her, and knowing she'd have to listen to Fermine's singing until the rains started, put her to bed.

"But now you have nothing to do *except* listen to him," I said.

"I tune him out completely. Once the rains come, he'll go back to grinding corn and mending tools."

"But, are you sick?"

"No, just surviving."

This was the way we lived until the morning of my birthday. I woke up to the gentle patter of rain on the roof. Fermine's house was silent. Mom was dressed and wrapping my present. She gave me a bottle of Chanel No. 5, so large it must have taken a week's welfare money. The most wonderful thing about the perfume was that it would profoundly shock our social worker if she ever found out. Actually, I really liked the smell of Yardley's English Lavender better, but the gold atomizer bottle was delirious. So was the fact that Mom would think of buying me something *that* fabulous. Most of the people I knew had parents who gave them warm jackets or petticoats for their birthdays, something they'd have to buy anyway.

My father's present turned out to be more along that line. He'd sent me a typewriter, which certainly was useful and expensive but a little too clearly the kind of present a man might send a fourteen-year-old daughter he thought of as a grind. And he was right.

For example, boys who asked my best friend, Dolly, to cut school and go fishing, asked me for the loan of my algebra homework.

Dolly said my first mistake was doing "every stick" of my homework, and the second mistake was letting anyone know I got good grades. The trick was to get the B average you needed to get into college without letting it slip up to the A– that plastered you all over the honor roll. Dolly managed this, but, unfortunately, I was one of those strange people who actually liked to study and, furthermore, got queasy feelings walking to school without my homework.

The funny part about the typewriter was that it *would* have made sense for Dolly, who was at least writing a novel. She was doing the story of her life and wanted to see how it looked in print. She said she positively yearned for the feel of typewriter keys under the tips of her fingers, and she was quite excited when the rain stopped and I was able to take the typewriter to her grandparent's farm the following weekend.

Not that spending the weekend at Dolly's was unusual. I often spent Saturdays and Sundays at her house because she lived ten miles out in the country and neither of us was old enough to drive back and forth. There was no question of trading off since I didn't even have my own room and her grandparents would have taken one look at Mom and said no, anyway.

That particular Friday afternoon was warm, a reprieve from winter. We stepped off the school bus into mud a foot deep, and I faced the half mile of graveled path running up to Dolly's house with the awful feeling in the pit of my stomach that I'd have to lug that portable every inch of the way, even though I'd only brought it along for Dolly.

It wasn't because Dolly wanted to put me down or even because she was lazy, really, but more because she was a "beautiful blue-eyed Texas blond." Dolly was hardly the empty-headed stereotype her drawl suggested. Her mother and dad had both been killed in an automobile accident; she hated living with grandparents whose sole interest in life was keeping their farm clean; she was writing a book; and she was the best yogi in our school. Dolly was a *real* person, but the problem was that most people took one look and rushed to pick up all the typewriters in her life, if you know what I mean.

It was easier to carry the typewriter than change Scarlet O'Hara, as Rhett Butler found out, so I switched the machine to my other hand and started up the path, its rocky surface biting through my loafers. A piece of gravel got lodged under one instep, and I tried to walk on the outside of that foot to delay the time I'd have to stop and set my new present down to get scratched forever, in order to save myself from being lamed.

"Such a heavenly day, clouds like whitening mushrooms," Dolly sighed.

"Umph."

"You ever try to fly, I mean really and truly fly?"

I felt a slushiness and wondered if my foot was bleeding. My hand was going to sleep, too.

"I haven't tried flying in ages and ages. Isn't that downright sad, the way they've really clipped my wings. My spirit—but today——"

"Here, better let me take that."

I felt someone tugging at the typewriter and turned sharply. I found myself face to face with Allan Sebastian. Allan, the bird freak, was darkly towering over me, his brown eyes looking down into mine. He was so close I could see stubble on his chin and feel his breath coming in short gasps, possibly from running to catch up. I could feel his hand over mine on the typewriter handle, dry and calloused and warm. Once, when someone had brought a seagull with a broken wing to school, I had watched him set it, and I saw his hands setting that wing as he reached for the typewriter. I dared not look down to where that hand actually touched mine.

Allan Sebastian! Allan Sebastian was the boy who lived on the farm next to Dolly's. We spent entire weekends watching him plow, walk, play with his collie, take the cows out to pasture in the morning and bring them back from pasture under the sunset. He had seven shirts, which he wore in rotation. His mother probably lined them up in his closet and he simply reached for one every morning. That was the way he was. He always looked neat, but he wasn't the kind of boy who just *had* to have the latest style shirt. Unfortunately for Dolly, he wasn't all that interested in girls either. He apparently preferred the company of animals, particularly birds, though he always said "hello" when we got off the bus together on the Fridays I came out. That was pretty nice, I thought, considering that he was nearly sixteen.

Dimly I heard, over the screech of spinning wheels, kids whistling and calling my name and Allan's as the school bus left. They had seen us, so it must be Allan tugging at my typewriter! What should I do?

"Here, better let me take that. Let go," he said, laughing.

"Let go?" I was jelly. I couldn't move. Then I must have stepped hard on the foot with the gravel because I felt a sudden shock of pain and I did let go. The typewriter fell in the mud. We both looked down at the shiny black case sinking into the oozing muck. It had struck the edge of the path and was listing over into the mire along the edge.

"I'm so sorry," I whispered finally.

"Damn!" he said, grabbing the muddy machine and running up the path. I would have liked to die, of course, but I concentrated on not throwing up.

"That boy is so clumsy he'd stumble over his very

own feet," Dolly said, chuckling. "Doesn't he just stalk along like one of his precious birds, stiff-legged as a sandpiper?"

"Come on, we can't keep him waiting."

"I only hope that little old machine of yours still works."

"Come on!"

"I have a ferocious headache, I mean a migraine for sure, and the very last person on this whole earth for whom I would run in the best of health is Allan Sebastian."

"Typewriters *can* be repaired, you know," I said witheringly, dumping the gravel out of my shoe. Two vicious pieces. No wonder. I started up the path.

"It will be all over school Monday," Dolly said softly, dragging after me, slowing me down.

"What?" All I needed was the entire school laughing at me because I dropped a typewriter.

"It will be all over school, silly, that Allan Sebastian carried April Mitchell's new typewriter home from school. Maybe it will even make the society page. Cheer up, it *could* be the start of something. You're sadly lacking in experience, you know," Dolly said, squeezing my arm.

"The start of Allan thinking I'm the dumbest female alive."

"Which means he *knows* you're alive. Besides, boys like their girls dumb. It's less threatening."

18

"Dolly, he's already *there*—and waiting—please hurry!"

"Rush, rush," Dolly replied, keeping an even pace. I would have looked like a fool running off and leaving her, and she knew it. *And* enjoyed the knowing. In the beginning, when Dolly first came to school, it had seemed like a miracle that I finally had a friend who understood me, who thought about life as a whole; but sometimes lately I felt she used this insight to get her own way a little too often.

Allan crouched by Dolly's gate, cleaning off the case with a newspaper. When he finished, he leaned the typewriter on a cross bar and stood watching us.

"Lascivious," Dolly muttered.

"What?"

"Never mind. At least he's cleaned off the case. But I aim to find out if it still works, poor Humpty-Dumpty."

"I could care less," I said coldly.

"Obviously."

He switched to scanning the sky as we came up, his hand shielding brown eyes against the sudden glare. Maybe watching a hawk? Allan kept an infirmary for wounded birds; everyone at school brought them out to him and, when the time came, he let the birds go at just the right place to rejoin their flocks. He wanted to be a veterinarian. He probably already knew more than most of them.

Dolly snapped open the typewriter case and began

examining it, right on the gravel.

"Thank you," I said ignoring her rudeness. Then, since he was still looking at the sky, "Isn't it a glorious day?"

Allan watched Dolly trying the keys and then turned and looked at me, really looked at me for the first time. I looked back. He was six feet tall, on the lanky side, and he had a big mouth, a long nose and his face was a man's face. His eyes—they were brown—and sad.

"I'm afraid it's going to rain again," he said. "One more rain like that last devil will wash out every pea seed on the ranch. A month's work. And, if we have to replant, we'll lose the early market, the only chance for decent prices—probably won't even make expenses."

"Grandaddy says folks have to be greedy to plant early, anyhow." Dolly rolled a sheet of paper into the typewriter.

Allan flushed deep red. He stood there clenching and unclenching one hand, looking ready to bolt. I *had* to stop him. I couldn't see him go, hating us.

"Dolly, Allan's probably worried about your grandparents' fields, too."

"I thought that was *your* typewriter," Allan said, smiling at me, his hands relaxing.

"Oh, but I'm not a novelist."

"That's good. At least I can understand you. A guy needs a dictionary to get those big words Dolly tosses

20

off." Allan hesitated and then spoke again. "Say, I met your mother the other day, down by the creek———"

I froze. "What was she doing?"

"Just watching the birds. First grownup I've ever seen who could sit still long enough to see birds. I mean she really likes them. Told me about the owls who live across from your house in the eucalyptus trees. You're sure lucky—she's really great. Maybe you like birds, too? Maybe you don't—but if you'd like to come see the birds in my infirmary—sometime."

"Oh, I'd love to," I said automatically. It was hard to concentrate when inside I just kept saying over and over that Allan liked Mom, liked the way she looked and the way she was. I had never invited kids to our house because everything was such a mess. But maybe Allan———

I looked up just in time to see Allan disappearing toward his own white frame house.

"Talk about shy Southern maidens," Dolly giggled.

"I should have asked him when, shouldn't I?"

Dolly shrugged, tossing her long blond hair back over her shoulders in a quick movement that meant she was annoyed. She snapped the typewriter case closed and stood up. Waiting. To see if I would pick it up?

"Not that you care, but I don't think it's broken. Oh, come on, April, it's not like he was asking you for a date and you could say, how about seven-thirty? When he says sometime, he's just being nice because your mother likes birds, that's all. I would have died on the spot if you'd opened that flapping mouth and asked that boy *when*. Let's hurry. My hair's frizzing up and that means rain." Dolly grabbed up the typewriter, turned on her heel, and left me standing alone, the taunting lilt in her voice still swinging in the air.

A cloud passed over the sun, darkening the muddy fields. I shivered. If Dolly hadn't taken the typewriter, I would have turned around and gone home. I didn't care about the typewriter but, somehow, the fact that she *had* taken it and lugged it to her house committed me to the weekend.

It did rain all that night and all the next day. I could see Allan digging trenches through the field, bent almost double by the driving storm, but I was careful not to let Dolly see me watching. Monday morning I left her the typewriter because I knew I'd drop it again if he asked about carrying the thing. As it turned out, he didn't come to school at all the next week. Dolly said she saw lanterns out in the fields until she went to sleep every night.

At home our roof leaked and the welfare worker, Susan Morgan, brought oil drums to catch the water. The drums crouched around the house like a dozen sleeping bullfrogs. The house creaked, and the fireplace, our only heat, belched clouds of smoke and ashes.

Between storms Fermine would climb over the roof trying to make emergency repairs, which were largely futile because the roof never dried out enough for any mastic to take. So the roof continued to leak, and Fermine stomped over it like a premature Santa Claus.

"Don't bother about the roof. It doesn't matter," Mom said to Fermine one evening as he warmed his hands before our fireplace.

"Then why have you stayed in bed all week?" Fermine asked, blowing at the smoking fire.

"It's warmer in bed. Ah, well, Fermine, does it really matter? We're all waiting for the daffodils, anyhow," Mom said, lighting a cigarette. She took a couple of puffs and slowly, deliberately, she blew three perfect smoke rings. They hovered delicately in the air between us, and we all watched them expand and drift away. The smoke rings seemed to make Fermine mad.

"How about if they lock you up? Then what? First you stay in bed, healthy as a horse, but all day you lie there reading. All right, stupid, lazy, but all right. But pretty soon, Mary, pretty soon you get up in the night and go for those crazy long walks. Don't shake your head at me! I know what I say. How many times the last two years you get unhappy and go out——"

"Please, please, Fermine, don't shout. It is a crime to go for a walk?" Mom sat up in the bed with her hands over her ears.

The old man stroked his beard nervously as he and my mother stared at each other. Abruptly he turned and strode to the door and stood there with his hand on the knob. "April, remember what the sheriff said last time? You get your mother up, hear?" he shouted, slamming the door behind him. I could hear his boots sucking at the mud between our yard and his own, and then I heard the cow bell on his gate. It would be warm in his house. I turned around and there was Mom, sitting there watching me, frowning.

"So?" I asked.

"Fermine's right. You do take care of me."

"Fermine's changed. He never used to be so nosy— or old—but at least there's always something to eat at his house," I said, looking in our cupboard, which was full of empty soda cracker boxes.

"Soon you'll get married and leave me," she whispered.

"Mo-ther! I happen to be fourteen years old, if you care to remember." Still, it was a flattering idea. At least *she* didn't think I was going to be an old maid.

"Just Juliet's age."

"Why don't you just get up and go to the store? I would very much appreciate something decent for supper for a change." I said it, though I knew it was pouring rain, over a mile to the store, and that, furthermore, the store had been closed for almost two hours.

"Tomorrow. Get me up when you go to school. What would you like most in the whole world for dinner?" Mom was looking at me dreamily, considering great meals. "Lobster?"

"No, what I'd really like is a full course chicken

dinner, complete with green salad and a roll with butter and honey. Not margarine, real butter." I stood
looking into the cupboard. We certainly had a lot of
canned milk and coffee, but not much else. I started
pushing cans around and found some clam chowder.
It was still there because it was the wrong brand, the
kind that tasted like flour paste, but it would have to
do.

"About the chicken, is that a promise?" I asked,
opening the can.

"Cross my heart and hope to die. Maybe we could
even go to the restaurant. Would you like that?"

3

THE WEDNESDAY BEFORE CHRISTMAS I STOOD IRON-
ing blouses and suddenly I had a good feeling, as if
every trouble had lifted and I was truly part of the
day. Our room, with a Christmas tree in the corner,
the crackling fire, and my mother sitting on the bed
wrapping presents, that was my life, and it might not
be Heaven but it wasn't Hell, either. I was glad to be
there.

I must have sighed, because Mom came over and laid
an arm around my shoulder. In those days that kind of
touching made me withdraw, but that afternoon I set
the iron on its haunches and leaned against her for a
moment. She'd been up all day, and that in itself was
encouraging. Maybe I wouldn't be out combing the

countryside for her *that* Christmas as I had been the year before. Besides, the fire was drawing well, it had stopped raining, and we'd even set the oil drums out in the back yard, so we had the house to ourselves again.

"When a girl sighs like that, it must be a young man," she said, peering down at me with her big gold-rimmed glasses askew, as usual.

I reached up and straightened them and then, pushing her gently away, I attacked my blouse with the cooling iron.

"No, probably just Christmas," I said. And yet, down under everything else, didn't Allan have a lot to do with feeling good? Not that *he* knew I was alive. In fact, since the typewriter incident, he had avoided me like the plague. I thought of him, though, and he was like a good dream.

"If only you'd tell me what you'd *really* like for Christmas, I wouldn't worry so," my mother added.

"You mean you haven't gotten my present yet? Come on, surprise me!" I tried to keep my voice light because I didn't want her to know there *was* something, the only present I'd really wanted in years, one even Mom would know was impossible. Welfare just did not pay for ballet lessons. If I could work in the fields the next summer, picking beans or drying apricots, then, maybe——

"You'll wear that blouse out in one ironing, April. Are you sure there isn't something, something magic you'd like for Christmas? Those are the only presents worth getting for someone as special as you."

She was quiet then. She seemed to be considering possible gifts because from time to time she'd shake her head impatiently. I put some wood on the fire and returned to the ironing. Above the fire and the hiss of the iron, I heard the owls in the eucalyptus trees across the street. My mother must have heard them, too.

"I was telling a friend of yours about those owls. Did I mention it? A lovely boy, and he wants to come and see them—I can't remember his name—are you blushing, April?" She broke off and watched me intently.

"Can't you ever keep those glasses on straight? Here, let me clean them, too. I can't imagine how anyone, no matter how nearsighted she may be, can see better in anything as dirty as *your* glasses. There, that's better," I complained, adjusting the glasses furiously.

"You *are* blushing!" she went on, smiling. "Well, you have good taste. Such a sensitive young man—and those beautiful hazel eyes. He said the owls ate field mice."

"Mother, he is merely a boy who lives next door to Dolly. He is nothing special." So his eyes weren't just brown, they were hazel. I liked that.

"I think he must be *very* special."

"I mean, after all, he's just a friend. Allan Sebastian. You'd like him though. He does most of the work on their farm—he's already saved their pea crop, for example. And you know how he feels about birds. Did

28

he tell you he's going to be a veterinarian?" Actually, I was glad the subject of Allan had come up. I had always told my mother about my friends. She knew almost as much about Dolly as I did, even though they'd never met. I never brought people to the house, and Mom never questioned it, but, until Allan, I had always told her about everyone. It was as if she knew Dolly and the others without having to go through the formality of meeting them and making them peanut butter sandwiches.

"He must think a good deal of you to confide in you."

"No, he tells everyone. Don't forget to wrap the tobacco you got for Fermine."

I watched her trying to roll the large can in tissue paper. A bed with rumpled blankets didn't make the best surface, but she finally got it all together and tied the ends with ribbon, gold at one end and silver at the other. When she looked up, she was smiling.

"I just got a wonderful idea," she said. "Why don't you have a Christmas party for your friends?"

I stared. She couldn't be serious.

"Here?" I asked, shocked. "I mean, we don't even have enough dishes."

"We could decorate with pine boughs. Fermine has a punch bowl. And I could meet your friends. I've always wanted to." She looked dreamy, as if she were remembering some fantastic ballroom and her waltzing in the prince's arms.

"Oh, but you've already met Allan. And he said he'd come see the owls someday," I said quickly, feeling trapped. Of course, decorations *could* hide a lot. It might even be fun to decorate and just have Dolly. But anything else was impossible. I hardly knew Allan, and anyone else would laugh. It wouldn't work. I guess she could see how I felt, because I watched the delight drain out of her face, leaving it blank. And that was worse than having the party. I took her hands.

"Mom, why don't we just ask Dolly? I'd like to have—Dolly really wants to meet you. Mom, can I invite Dolly? Mom?" I glanced around the room, desperately looking for something to make her glad again, to bring back the Christmas feeling, something stupendous.

"Mom, Mo-ther, do you really want to know what I want for Christmas, what I've wanted for the last three years?"

She did look up then, and I plunged on, knowing it was a crazy thing to do but unable to stop myself.

"What I want, really want, is to be a ballerina. I'd love lessons, even one lesson."

"Ah, so lovely," she nodded. "But one lesson—you need ten years of lessons," she whispered, and there were tears in her eyes.

The next morning she was gone. I saw that she had not slept in her bed and felt a familiar sinking in the pit of my stomach. I'd known I shouldn't tell her about the ballet lessons. I'd known, and yet I'd rushed

30

headlong into asking for something totally impossible, knowing that Christmas was the gloomiest time of the year for Mom. Of course, maybe she'd just gone to the store. I *had* to go to school. We'd be in for real trouble with the social worker if I didn't.

When she was still not home that afternoon, I started out to hunt for her.

4

IT MUST HAVE BEEN MIDNIGHT AT LEAST, AND AT LAST I'd returned to the creek where Allan had met her. I fell back into the willows, keeping perfectly still, listening over my own heart for the footstep I might not hear. I couldn't seem to stop panting. I should have stayed home. A tramp jungle was no place for a fourteen-year-old girl, especially in the middle of the night. Why *did* I always go running out like that when I never found her? I wondered.

Actually, I knew perfectly well why I had been running all night. I could hear Fermine's voice warning me to keep Mom away from the sheriff. And I could hear the nasal whine of the sheriff's voice above my pulses, above the wind and the highway traffic.

"Next time I see that mother of yours walking zombie around this town, I swear to God I'll lock her up," he'd said. "You mark my words, girl, that mother of yours is a menace. Why, she could just as well start a fire and burn the whole town down."

How would he know, a man they called Gopher because he was so near blind? But he was our sheriff and he'd lock her up. That was no bluff.

Better get going. My heart felt better, but there was a cramp in my stomach. So quiet in the willows with the hoboes and dogs and birds all sleeping. What was the song she always used to sing about the willows?

In a tree by a willow a little bird sat,
Singing, "Willow, tit-willow, tit-willow,"
And I said to him, "Birdy dear, why do you sit
Singing willow, tit-willow, tit-willow?
Is it a weakness of intellect, birdie," I cried,
"Or a rather tough worm in your little inside?"

What was that? Heavy steps, not hers. I lay perfectly still. The footsteps hesitated, stopped a few feet away. I waited. Waited. They started again, heavy on one foot, coming closer, brisker, faster. My throat was dry.

Then the steps went on by. I heard them gradually dimming as whoever it was took the path down by the creek that ran along the railroad track. Must be a tramp. Lots of drifters camped down there.

I waited. Silence. Then I scrambled up, sliding off

the willow branches, and ran to the highway. I didn't look back. It was dark along the highway, and I kept stumbling into the ditch that ran alongside. There was no question of running any more, even if I didn't have the cramp, because I didn't want to attract attention. In the dark, wearing Levis, I might be just another tramp and tramps never ran.

I was heading for town. She liked the town at night; the houses and people were at rest, she said. Fog was coming in from the ocean, and it swirled around the few lights still burning, gradually closing in, so that it was difficult to judge the distance. It couldn't be more than half a mile, though. As the fog got thicker, the lights blended so that the town looked like one glowing ball. Out to sea I could hear the mourning triple blast of the fog horn. Otherwise the night was silent, except for my own footsteps and my breathing.

Suddenly a spotlight hit me. I jerked around and my hands flew over my eyes. The light blinded me. I sank to my knees in the ditch, cowering in freezing mud. The sheriff? And, as abruptly as it came, the blasting light was gone. Only a passing car. What did I expect on a highway? I climbed out of the ditch, scraped at the mud caking on my Levis, and trudged on.

It wasn't until I finally got to town and stood under a streetlight that I knew how cold I was. But I didn't have the sense to go on home, even then. I knew I couldn't find her but I had to know if the sheriff had gone to bed. I had to know if she was free of him for a few hours.

His house was black and silent. In fact there wasn't a light on all along his street, and the nearest street-light was at least half a block away, down on the corner. I stood there thinking of all those people snoring away in double beds, not liking us when they *were* awake, and then of the sheriff not even knowing how he'd kept me awake all night. He was inside that little white house with the twin patches of lawn edged in abalone shells and he never had to be afraid, the blind old bully.

The fog had begun to come in seriously, gradually enveloping the sheriff's whole house, but, even so, those abalone shells glowed like empty moons. They were set so evenly that moving one abalone shell would wreck the whole effect. I wondered if old Gopher Grodin had a dog. How strange it was that I didn't even know if he had a dog, the man who was chasing us.

I'd have to work quickly. I stooped down and took up half a dozen shells, brushing off two slugs, and laid them on the lawn. There should be enough to make it the size of the whole lawn. What would he do if he caught me? What would he do if he didn't and just came out and found them on his way to work tomorrow?

Soon I had the first letter, which needed about fifty

shells. I took the next shells from the lawn on the other side of the concrete walk, being careful not to crack one against the other. It pleased me that when he first came out in the morning he'd be mad as soon as he saw that someone had tampered with his lawn, with his even row of abalone shells. He'd be even madder when he found out what it said. There wasn't anyone in town who said NO to Gopher Grodin. I meant it, too! He wasn't going to ruin our lives. I wasn't going to let him, not that he'd ever know who had talked back. He'd go around sniffing and end up suspecting everyone he met. Maybe he'd even get ulcers.

When I was done, I had a hard time leaving. The abalone shells gleamed in the fog. I was hypnotized by their message. No one had ever done anything like that in all the years he'd been there, and that dated back to before I was born. Well, it was about time. I wanted to hide in the bushes and see the expression on his near-sighted face when he read the word in the morning, but I couldn't. I had to see if Mom was home. I had done it for her. I took one more look at the shimmering NO outlined in shells on the clipped lawn, threw a kiss, and turned and ran.

I was still laughing over my trick on the sheriff as I turned down the alley that ran along the back of our house. It was dark, but there was already the feel of morning in the cold air, the hint of grey and red over the hushed sky. I shoved my hands deep into my Levi pockets and rubbed them against the new rough denim, trying to get warm. I scuffed my sandals into the sandy alley, but the sand was dewy, cold, and grainy between my toes. It would be worth it, though, if I could only see the look on Gopher's face when he tried to make out what had been done to his precious abalone shells. I'd go see, in spite of the risk, except for our social worker. I *had* to go to school. I could not risk that prissy lady's coming to look for me. She had tried to put me in a foster home the last time Mom had gone for a walk. We weren't neat enough for her.

I heard the roosters and then the dogs answering them. The roosters woke the dogs, and then their owners had to let them out in order to get that last hour of sleep. Everyone in town, except us, had roosters, and they were welcome to them, meanest birds on earth, always eating, always complaining. The noise was bad news because if the other dogs were out, Thor most likely was out, too. Thor, the meanest Doberman in the world, had lived on our block for two years, and his dearest wish in the world was to take a chunk out of my leg. I knew I was too tired to stop him.

There was a rustling in the bushes behind me. Thor? I stopped. No sound. Then the faintest whishing, whishing, the sort of sound a dog might make skirting a bush or brushing his tail across it. Thor wouldn't bark or growl. I froze. He hadn't seen me yet. Should I run for it? I'd never make it. Maybe——

Then I saw him stand up, a dark hulk against the lightening sky. Fermine, not Thor. It was only Fermine out killing snails! I could see his straw hat and the grey hair and full beard and the brass buttons on his overalls and the salt box in his outstretched hand. Fermine did not believe in poisons of any kind and he did believe that a man must do his own dirty work, so he got up before dawn and sprinkled salt on the slugs in his garden. When I was little, I had set my alarm so I could help him.

Fermine looked up, and I ducked behind our garbage can. I wanted to call out and go with him to the warmth of his old wood stove. He'd ask me to breakfast, and we'd have tortillas filled with jack cheese and sweet chilies. And cocoa. But he would also ask what I was doing out at such an hour. Mom didn't like Fermine coming after her when she went out on walks, not since he had gotten the idea of marrying her.

I had my breakfast with Fermine every morning before that, and no one ever said I should stop, but it was funny how I started to notice things after Mom wouldn't marry him. His false teeth didn't fit, and sometimes he'd smack his lips over a good bite and the drool would run down the side of his mouth. Little things. Could he help when he was born? Ridiculous. Still, I had stopped going. Fermine never said anything. He probably saw me standing there, but unless I gave a sign, he'd mind his own business. That was the way he was.

My knees felt locked in their crouch, waiting for Fermine to go back in the house. Thor would get me

38

yet. And maybe Mom was back? Finally, I heard his screen door slam, and I made a mad dash for our back door, running an obstacle course through the piles of bottles I was going to turn in for money someday.

The door was open. Maybe she was back.

"Mom, hey, are you home?" I knew before I turned on the light that she wasn't back yet. The light from the window fell on our beds, still rumpled just as we'd left them the morning before. The book she'd been reading lay face down on the blankets. *David Copperfield*, an English assignment of mine. An ashtray and an empty coffee cup and a pack of cigarettes lay on the floor next to her bed. Her jacket was on the floor, too. I hadn't noticed she'd forgotten that. She must be freezing. She always needed more clothes than I did.

I stood in the doorway looking at her empty bed as daylight spread over our town, and I began to wish that I hadn't been so clever with the sheriff's abalone shells. He might not know they were my bright idea, but they weren't going to make him very peaceful that day with anyone he caught wandering around town "zombie like."

5

It was still foggy when I got to school, so the other kids seemed like figures in a blurry painting, maybe Degas' ballet dancers, framed away from me by the fact that somewhere out in that pea soup the sheriff might come upon my mother. He'd jail her without bail after finding that abalone NO on his front lawn. I stood on the playground considering whether I should call Fermine. She'd asked me never to bother him but surely she'd rather have him find her than the sheriff. I had to stay in school or we'd have the Welfare Department as well as the sheriff hounding us. Of course, if Gopher Grodin didn't sniff around like a pack of bloodhounds, we wouldn't be in such a mess. Mom would come back in a few days. She came home when she could. She didn't hurt anyone, so why didn't he leave her alone?

I decided to call Fermine and started across the courtyard toward the attendance office, ducking behind an oak tree when Dolly and her new boyfriend and Allan got off their bus. I didn't feel up to seeing them today. For one thing, Dolly even wrote about her mother and dad's car accident, and I didn't want her writing about Mom and me. And what would they say if they knew where I'd been all night?

They were about the only kids at school who *would* care where I'd been. Since my experience with Girl Scouts, I'd learned to keep my friendships strictly casual and only at school, except for Dolly, who understood. I'd liked being in Girl Scouts, even if I didn't have a uniform, until I saw that each meeting was held at a different member's house. Naturally, the girls compared houses, mothers, refreshments, even bathrooms. I suppose they would have made an exception in my case, but it was easier to quit than explain.

Even with Dolly, I tried to keep my distance. The first time she'd invited me out to her place, I had come right out and said I couldn't have her back because my mom was sick a lot. She said fine, because sick folks frazzled her anyway. Dolly was really sensitive; but even she wouldn't have understood then about searching all night.

I shook my head and reached down into my purse.

Fortunately there was a dime and the booth was empty. I dialed Fermine's number quickly in case Dolly and Allan had seen me. There might not be much time. I turned my back to the crowded hall and listened to the rings on the other end of the line. He was probably still in the garden.

He hated the phone because it could interrupt anything a man did, so I knew he wouldn't hurry to answer. He was probably cleaning off his shoes before he went in the house. Stomping on the door mat. Another ring and he'd pick up the phone. But he didn't. The phone kept on and on, and there was no answer. He must be over hoeing asparagus. Fermine owned a small farm on the edge of town. If he wasn't home early in the day, he was almost always there; and in December he'd be hoeing asparagus or Chinese peas. No phone.

The tardy bell rang and I slammed out of the booth. About third period the teachers' voices all began to take on the sheriff's nasal twang. Faces blurred, the mixture of sweat and perfume and chewing gum became overpowering. The rooms were hot and close. Once I woke myself by opening a window and leaning out into the fog. Finally the last bell rang, releasing me from an unsuccessful struggle to stay awake through the American Revolution.

Fifteen minutes later I stood in our living room calling for Mom. She wasn't home. Fermine still wasn't home. I wondered if I should wait for him. We could cover more ground with the car. It would be dark in two hours. At least I should leave a note.

I suddenly felt terribly tired and very much alone. If only Fermine would come home so I could ask him what to do. If only I could take a little nap, but there was so little time, two hours until dark. The house smelled of mildew and rotten fruit. I threw open the windows and, leaning out, breathed deep of the lavender hedge. Like smelling salts, the lavender began to revive me.

I would wait for Fermine. I knew my mother wasn't home, and yet I started making afternoon coffee for both of us. I did it leisurely. She liked hobo coffee; that is, she liked the grounds boiled with the water in an open pot and then left a minute to sink to the bottom under a shot of cold water and an egg shell. I toasted two slices of Fermine's home ground wheat bread, then rinsed out two mugs and poured the coffee; the fragrance steamed the room.

She liked to sit up on her bed and hear about school while we snacked, so I set the food on a small table by her bed. Then I lay back, propped against the red velvet sofa pillows.

Sometime during the night I cried, and the wetness on the pillow bothered me fitfully. I knew there was some reason to get up, but I could not recall what it was.

Finally I opened my eyes.

"Oh. God, the house is on fire," I screamed. Then

I realized it wasn't the house but the sky that was scarlet, burning over the eucalyptus windbreak. No smoke. I looked again and saw the sunrise flooding the sky. Mom faced her bed toward the east so she could see the sunrise. She said she liked to celebrate the morning. But how did it get to be morning?

It's the sheriff, I thought, when I heard a familiar man's voice. She'd counted on me and I'd let her down. I lay huddled in the blankets, fighting the temptation to pull the covers back over my head. My nose and ears tingled in the frosty dawn. I kept thinking it was too late and at the same time that if I could just close my eyes for another five minutes I might come up with some solution.

The kitchen door scraped open. It warped with the first rains every winter and opening it required some strength. He must be standing there staring at our one room ghetto. I wondered how long it would take blind old Gopher to find me under the tangled bed covers.

"Ah, there's my baby. Isn't she beautiful?" I heard my mother ask. So she wasn't in jail. Maybe he couldn't find a charge. Well, I didn't need his opinion of my looks.

"She'd better get moving or she'll be late for school." It wasn't the sheriff but only Fermine. I could hear my mother's rich warm voice again, and Fermine answering her, and they both turned bitter in my ears. I knew, without uncovering my head, without forcing open my eyes, how Mom would look. That "isn't life wonderful" look would be written all over her face. Fermine would look peaceful, dead tired, and relieved. But she had left no note when she walked out, nor had he left me a note when he went to find her. Neither of them worried about me.

"Maybe I should make her some breakfast?" This time the voice, soft and a woman's, did belong to a stranger. How many troups had they brought along this time. She always had to bring people home.

I dashed for the shower without looking back, clutching the blankets around me like mummy wrapping, slamming the door and locking it behind me. How I loathed them all. I didn't trust myself to speak or I'd have told them so. Then I stood under the hot water, turned on full so it pelted me hard with soothing warmth, so it drowned out the voices, turning round slowly so the cold outside could not penetrate. Soon I was soaped and clean and the bathroom warmed with the steam, and still I stood under the shower, relaxing until the thirty gallon tank emptied, and the cold water brought goosepimples.

"At least she's home. We've lucked out again," I said.

I opened the bathroom door to the smell of fresh cocoa and of eggs frying in butter and to the odor of Fermine's bread toasting. There was a crackling fire, and the room was already warm. Outside the scarlet sunrise had paled to a barely ripe watermelon color. The birds and roosters and dogs were awake, proud and furious and loud. I listened for Thor, but couldn't hear him.

There was only one stranger, a girl of about twenty who stood at the stove, turning eggs. She looked remarkably like my mother and I remembered that this had been true of two other women who had brought Mom home. Perhaps seeing someone in trouble who looked like themselves made them sympathetic, or maybe she sought them out. However it was, this girl had the same sad smile, the same sunken eyes and high cheekbones that made people ask if Mom had Indian blood. They were tall and bony, both of them. This girl might have been a sister to my mother, except that the girl was beautiful. She glowed where Mom sagged. Still, around town people sometimes told me my mother had been a real beauty, so maybe I was seeing her as she had been twenty years before.

I couldn't stop looking from one to the other. Then I saw Fermine, warming himself at the fireplace, looking from one to the other and then over to me. Did I look like them, too?

"I kept trying to find you," I growled at Fermine.

"I know. I kept meaning to come back and tell you I was looking," he said wearily.

"Aren't they both wonderful people?" Mom asked, pulling me to her with one arm and putting the other around the young woman's shoulder. I leaned against her a moment. She smelled of anise weed, so she must

46

have been sleeping out in the fields. I pulled back.

"The sheriff would have jailed you if he'd found you," I said.

"Mornin', little lady, and praise God for victory," the other woman said before Mom had a chance to answer.

"You're Jehovite?" Fermine asked.

"I am thankful at being able to serve our Lord. Just you set right down there, sir. Breakfast's about set." The woman patted my place with one hand while she put the eggs on the table with the other. She had long delicate fingers, and I noticed she bit her nails.

Then she wiped her hands on her apron and sat down. Everybody looked at the food. Mom seemed about ready to fall asleep. Fermine's eyes watered and he needed a shave. The stranger appeared to be in charge. Finally, I reached for a piece of toast, and instantly she started talking.

"May the sweet breath of our Lord Jesus bless this food from which we take the succor to serve you, Lord. We are jubilant this morning over this here woman being safely returned to her babe——"

She said more, but I was furious at being called a babe and worrying about that toast dangling out at the end of my hand, so I didn't hear her. Fermine grinned, but whether he knew how I felt about the description or whether he had almost reached for toast himself, I couldn't tell.

"The Lord provides. Amen."

The eggs were still hot, and the coffee scalded my

throat. Mrs. Pritchard, for that turned out to be her name, was as hungry as we were, and for a while we ate without speaking. I couldn't ask how or where Fermine had found Mom for fear of upsetting her again, and there didn't seem to be anything else to say. Mom was almost asleep and Fermine was sulking.

"Can I take you home, Mrs. Pritchard?" Fermine asked, and then added, "I'm taking you to school, April."

"That's kindly of you, sir, but I walk with God," she answered serenely.

Fermine and I looked at each other and shrugged. There was no point in asking if that meant she was moving in with us until we got converted. We knew my mother had invited other people.

"Just leave the dishes. I'll do them when I get home —and thanks, thanks a lot," I said, picking up books, jacket, and purse as I edged toward the door.

Mom was already asleep over her coffee. Mrs. Pritchard deftly removed a half-burned cigarette from between Mom's fingers and, smiling with my mother's sad smile, she shooed me out of my own door with the dishtowel.

I stumbled down the steps and across the back yard. Fermine sighed and followed me. We'd had people move in with us before, and sooner or later Fermine always had to kick them out.

"Well, why did you let her come back with you in the first place?" I growled.

6

Mrs. Pritchard was gone when I got home that afternoon. Nor did I ever see her again. An encampment of migratory workers moved on to the desert where they cut dates over the winter, and I suppose she must have gone with them. I wondered for a while whether she lived with a husband and maybe a baby, and if she were some distant relative. Gradually her face blurred until it became one with all the other soft-spoken women who had brought my mother home from walks.

Mom never mentioned her again, either. Possibly my mother did not like to remember that she ever left home. I'm not sure she *did* remember, so I never asked questions or brought up anything that might have rocked the boat. Like ballet lessons, for example. I decided if I could earn the money during the summer, we could talk about them again. Meanwhile I could practice at Dolly's.

We had a false spring in January that year, days so warm the trees bloomed while we sunburned on chaises in the back yard and listened to Fermine predict a summer without fruit. Then it was my mother who read and I who sat dreaming through the balmy afternoons. She was re-reading Dickens, and I'm sure he would have been pleased to see her laughing and crying over the dull stuff he wrote.

I was building conversations for the weekends when Allan would walk Dolly and me from the school bus to the gate separating their farms, conversations I was too tongue-tied to start when I had the chance. Allan Sebastian had turned sixteen and gotten his drivers' license. Dolly was sure he would ask me for a date, and I knew he would not. Dolly thought her grandparents might let her double date with us. She was already seeing a boy named Chris Roberts on the sly, having her grandfather drop her at the library to study and slipping out for a Coke, things like that, but so far her grandparents stuck to the too-young-to-date formula. Dolly figured they thought Allan was "sensible" enough to let her go with us. But that didn't mean Allan *wanted* to date me. Still, basking under the January sun, it seemed at least possible.

Then the weather shifted, bringing Fermine's black

frost and high winds which stripped the blooming fruit trees, scattering wasted blossoms. It was cold, too cold. One afternoon on the brink of rain, I was hurrying home to build a fire and huddle in front of it. I must have caught the school flu because I ached all over and my head throbbed at each step. So I pushed against the wind, counting the blocks. How I yearned to get home, and how I hoped my mother had a fire going!

It was not encouraging to see our front door swinging loose, banging its frame, like the entrance to a deserted house. I ran down the gravel path with the wind blowing eucalyptus leaves ahead of me through the living room and, as I saw then, through the open kitchen door out into the back yard.

But Mom *was* home. She was propped up against her red velvet sofa pillows on the bed, wrapped in a grey Army blanket, with her feet dangling over the side of the bed. She kept rubbing one instep against the other, and I noticed she was wearing my gym socks. She hunched against the wind, which whipped her hair across her face so I couldn't see her expression, but she seemed to be watching three old women who were kneeling by her feet, singing "Rock of Ages." Their voices had the grating sound of an old wind-up phonograph.

The women looked identical. Bulging eyes and pursed blue lips popped out of wrinkled faces surrounded by tight grey permanents. I believe their clothes were also grey. They were all scowling at me, though I had never seen any of them before.

"What's with the Greek Chorus?" I asked wearily, closing the door. It was no day to put up with more of Mom's old women fanatics. "Wait, let me get some aspirin first."

"All I wanted was a cup of coffee," Mom said, brushing back her hair and tying it with a black shoe lace. She didn't know what was going on either. I'd have to get rid of them, as usual.

"So, okay. I'll make some—but not for them."

The singing stopped. We stood looking at one another in the sudden quiet until the kitchen door slammed, releasing us.

"Don't you dare turn on that stove!" the women screamed in unison.

"This is my house, and I'll turn on the stove if I want to."

"Just a minute——"

There, in the open front doorway, stood our social worker, Miss Susan Morgan, bracing herself against the doorframe as if there were an earthquake and looking blankly around the room without focusing on any of us. She always looked as if she were trying to decide where to step next. Which left the rest of us waiting to see if she had finished what she had to say or if there was more coming. You were never sure with her when any conversation was over. I don't know how many times I've thought she was listening and I'd be talking away only to have her drift out the front door and drive off in her little sports car, leaving me with my mouth hanging open.

"What brings you here—it isn't Monday, is it?" I asked because the silences were getting to me. She came one Monday a month, and we suffered through her visits because we needed the welfare money.

"Oh, we're so glad you've come!" the women chorused.

"Your mother called me, April, asked me to come —but what is all this, what's going on here? Mary, you sounded—so strange. Are you all right?" Miss Morgan was finally looking at Mom.

"I only wanted to make a cup of coffee," Mom said, shrugging and indicating the three women at her feet.

"We got here just in the nick of time."

"Another five minutes and I hate to think."

"I couldn't have been responsible."

"Who are you?" Miss Morgan asked the old women, taking a few tentative steps toward them and fixing them with her big blue eyes. This startled the women, maybe because Miss Morgan was young enough to be their granddaughter. She was very pretty, with long blond hair and a milky complexion and big gold-rimmed glasses that were always slipping so you couldn't believe they were really useful. Mom called her Alice in Wonderland. I'd liked her until she came by when Mom was out walking, got me to talk, and tried to put me in a foster home.

"Yes, who are you?" I asked.

"We've just saved her from suicide, is who we are!" One lady detached herself from the chorus, and her knees creaked as she stood up, pointing at Mom.

"Is *that* what you thought? Ah, no, I only wanted to make a cup of coffee."

"She turned on the burners and didn't light them and closed the windows and lay down to die!" the old woman was shouting.

"Ah, no, I only wanted to rest a moment—to get warm. You see the Hindus say if you take your life you have to live it all over. What would be the point?" Mom asked gently. The ladies stared.

"How many burners were on?" Miss Morgan asked quickly.

"Oh, come on, can't you see—Mom just forgot to light the stove. If you had gotten us a stove with an automatic pilot, this would never have happened." They were so funny, all of them trying to be important at Mom's expense, but it was more than two aspirin could handle. My head was going to explode. I had to have some tea. I went to the sink, filled a pan of water and lit the stove, tossing the burned-out match in the sink.

Suddenly, somebody grabbed me from behind. Strong bony fingers clawed at my clothes, raked across my breasts, punched me with a ring stone, and knocked me over, pulling me backwards onto the floor. Whoever it was smelled of a heavy sweet perfume and lay on top of me, until I felt I was drowning in the awful suffocating smell. I had to get up! We rolled over and over on the dirty floor, bumping into table legs, knocking over a chair.

I heard myself scream, my mother yelling for Miss Morgan to stop us, and the back door slamming. Still we rolled over and over, both grunting, my legs pinned by tough bony thighs and by heavy shoes repeatedly kicking at my shins. We paused at the same moment, and I stared at one of the old women. She was smiling. I was down rolling around the floor with somebody's crazy grandmother. This crazy old woman had watched too many westerns, I thought. I stared up into lacy cobwebs careening across our ceiling. It was covered with spider webs. All this time we'd been living in a den of spiders, probably tarantulas, and I never would have known if this grandmother hadn't jumped me.

"Get off of her, you!" Miss Morgan shouted.

"Who, me?" But then I saw that Miss Morgan was tugging at the old woman's coat.

"Thank God for your life," the woman said, pulling down her girdle as she climbed to her feet. She snapped off the stove and faced me. She looked excited, happy.

"I think I have a temperature," I said.

"Me, too," Miss Morgan agreed. "Well, get off the floor before you get pneumonia."

"We saved your mother's life and yours, too, and *this* is the thanks we get."

"It was a miracle we got here in time, a true miracle."

"Suicide. We came by on a Christian errand and——"

Their old voices blended and I could hardly pick out the one who had attacked me. She must be the one who sparkled, I decided, the one with pink cheeks. Tomorrow they'd be out in front of the post office telling everyone in town about it.

"I know. You sell magazine subscriptions." Now I remembered them. They supplemented Social Security checks by selling magazines, Christmas cards, and embroidered handkerchiefs. Fermine called them the three monkeys, said they could pour gossip out of an empty milk bottle. He had chased them with a pitchfork when he caught them picking his lavender. Fermine was leery of old women anyway, forever afraid they were plotting to marry him.

"Your *Redbook* subscription expires next month," the woman who jumped me said in a subdued voice.

"Do you suppose I forgot to light the stove?" Mom asked.

"There's a special if you renew for three years."

"I'm going to get Fermine. Mom, don't you dare renew our subscription," I said. Miss Morgan was closing doors and windows as I went into the windy twilight. It turned out that Fermine wasn't home; but returning, I saw the old women hurrying down the street, bent into the wind, three solitary figures taking the brunt of the coming storm. I knew they would spread their story all over town and that my mother would undoubtedly still buy magazines the next time they knocked on our door. And, though I might not recognize them on the street, they would point me out because they wanted to believe they were heroines and I was an ungrateful kid.

It would be dark soon. I could hear the birds twittering in the tall pines and along our eaves, and somewhere a cow lowed to be milked. I could hear the news commentators and see families at the dinner table through organdy curtained windows. Some houses were lighted, and then the street lights flared on, coming alive in the gathering dusk. I smelled stew and frying steak and biscuits. If only Miss Morgan would go, I could fix our dinner without her lecture on nutrition. She hadn't been much help, just tugging away at that old lady's coat.

"Funny old women," I said, laughing, stretching into the sky. The first stars were out.

Miss Morgan was straining coffee into three cups. Someone had turned on the lights and started a fire. Mom was sitting on the bed, stirring sugar into her coffee.

"I wouldn't have bothered you except that they were threatening to call the sheriff and they wouldn't tell me what was wrong," Mom said, shaking her head. "I know how busy you are, such a heavy responsibility."

"Please, I'm just doing my job. I get paid."

"Then why didn't you get us a stove with an automatic pilot like I asked. See, see what happens." I burst into the room. "I thought you were going to see about that stove."

"You have to wait your turn, just like all the rest of us, April. In the meantime, I think you'd better leave at least one window open all the time." Her eyes widened the way they did when she was mad, and the whites looked eerie in the firelight, reflecting the flames. I waited, but she didn't say anything more. She hesitated, considering, then shrugged and started picking up her things—the camel's hair coat, the long trailing scarf which she twisted around her finger when she was nervous, and the black briefcase. "I'd better be going. It's a long drive back to San Luis," she said, her voice flat.

"The wind is dying," I said.

"I'll try to get money for that stove. Just you see you go to school, April. Help your mother." She pulled the door closed, and I could hear her high heels crunching up the gravel path; a car door slammed and, finally, after a false start, her engine sprung to.

"Poor tired little girl. She even forgot her coffee," Mom said.

"Poor tired little girl? Don't you know she tried to put me in a foster home? Remember?" I screamed.

"And she will, too, if this keeps up. You're playing right into her hands."

"No one can take you away. You're my daughter. There's nothing to worry about," my mother said calmly, drinking her coffee.

7

"IF THIS IS APRIL, IT MUST BE FRIDAY," ALLAN TEASED as we got off the bus the next day. "Your mother's really fine to let you come out here on weekends. I'll bet she misses you."

"Yes, she is nice about it," I replied, ducking my head to hide burning cheeks. Allan was so psychic it was frightening. He couldn't have known I almost hadn't come because I was afraid of leaving Mom alone with the gas stove. That morning I'd even asked Fermine to check in. But how could Allan know I was thinking about Mom, unless we had some private ESP going for us? I wondered if he believed people could tune in on each other's minds.

"That is because April's mother does not have

chickens to feed or cows to milk or bean fields to weed or any of the other little chores that keep us chained to the farm and away from all civilization," Dolly said with feeling.

"Carry on, Doll, carry on! Last Saturday was the first time I've seen you with a hoe in a year. And April was out there hoeing with you."

"I don't mind," I said. Hoeing was better than wrestling with old ladies or getting rid of nosy social workers. Not that I'd want to make a career of hoeing, but it wasn't that bad.

"April doesn't mind hoeing because she thinks bending over is good for the leg muscles. But since I aspire to the art of writing and not to the dance it doesn't do one little thing for me."

"I do not aspire to *any* art. And you don't even *have* cows." Never again would I confide in Dolly about anything. It was stupid enough, wanting to dance when I'd never had a single lesson, without her bellowing about it from every rooftop. I knew I would die right on the spot if Allan asked me about it.

"That's right, there isn't a cow on your farm!" Allan said, grinning. Fortunately, he never let a chance to get the best of Dolly pass.

"Yet!"

The word hovered between us, and we were quiet as we dodged puddles in the oozing driveway. I tried to step only on the mounds of new grass, which might get my loafers wet but protected them from mud. Dolly would never milk a cow in her whole life. There was no need to worry about that! It was the silence that bothered me. I'd spent most of the week making up things I wanted to say to Allan, and none of them were right. If we mentioned the weather, Dolly thought Allan was blaming us for rain, and the very subject depressed him, because this had been a particularly rainy winter. I couldn't talk about home, and we always talked about school. We were halfway up the hill already. I looked up at Allan beside me, and he winked. I smiled. He pressed my hand so briefly I couldn't be sure it wasn't an accident. I couldn't look up again, either.

"The thing is," Dolly said, not noticing, "the thing is that Saturday is the only time I have to work on my book and I really think they give me chores just so I won't be able to. My grandmother thinks writing a novel is halfway between working crossword puzzles and making out with some guy."

"Like Chris Roberts, for example?" Allan asked.

"Like they would die if they knew that dumb football player existed." Dolly blushed. "But he's not the only trouble."

"I know what you mean," Allan agreed. "My birds don't lay eggs for breakfast, so as far as the folks are concerned, they're several cuts below chickens."

"But they were sure enough proud when the newspaper ran that article on your saving birds. They showed that little old paper all over the county. This badge of honor complex they all have is devastating. Absolutely. I mean, what's so great about looking back on seventy years of dusted tables?" Dolly spread her arms as if asking the sky.

"We don't dust tables or write books or save birds, either, and I wish we did," I muttered.

"You're lucky, and you don't even know it," Doll said, tossing her hair. "You are the last of the buffalo, and you don't know it."

"Which reminds me, how about coming over and seeing my birds tomorrow while Doll's pounding out the great American novel?"

"Oh yes, I'd like to! What time?" I asked with a sidelong glance at Dolly. She acted as if she hadn't heard, bent down and picked an early buttercup, looked up at the sky, and then stared straight ahead. Maybe it was wrong to ask about the time, but he'd asked me for tomorrow, and that was almost the same as a date, wasn't it?

"After breakfast," Allan said, and reached over and squeezed my hand before he branched off toward his place, whistling.

"Stop blushing like a greenhorn," Doll growled. "I told you he'd ask."

Early the next morning I saw Allan out in the far pasture with his dad and Dolly's grandfather. The older men were mending fence while Allan chased half a dozen cows back into their own pasture. No one said whose bean field they'd eaten. Nor did I care. What mattered was that Allan was busy and wouldn't be able to keep my first date. I'd been stood up before I'd ever gone out. It didn't look promising. I climbed back into bed and pretended to be asleep.

"Don't bother her, dear. She needs her sleep."

"Grandmother, there are many things in life that April needs more than sleep," Dolly answered, pushing open my door. "April, stop sulking! Your hero just phoned, and I told him you were on your way over. Now, hold it—get dressed first—for once in your life, relax—that doesn't mean making the bed—I'll do that. All right, you'll do—except for the ribbon. It makes you look like Judy in the *Wizard of Oz*. Now, go. Walk like a lady, dear. Remember, your first date may mean a real date for me, too." Dolly leaned against the windowsill with her arms crossed and a look of intolerable amusement on her face.

"You'll find him fooling with those birds of his," Allan's father said, pointing in the general direction of a weatherbeaten building that must have been, in better days, either a large shed or a small barn. The door was ajar, and I entered the dark musty cavern cautiously. It smelled damp and of manure and hay. At first I couldn't see anything; only gradually did I make out ledges running along each side on which sat cages of birds. Far down at the other end there was a skylight and a long counter with a double sink. Allan stood before the sinks with his back to me.

"Allan?" Someone had laid planks over the earth floor; they squeaked with each step I took toward him.

"Great. Did you have any trouble finding me? Say, do you mind giving me a hand here? The game warden brought in a pair of grebes, and they've picked up some oil. I'd like to get to them before the shock." Allan turned then, and I could see that he was holding a shiny black bird with a long neck and a yellow beak. It was wrapped in a towel. "I can show you around later," he added apologetically.

The bird and I stared at each other, and he didn't look friendly. I could see that his feathers were crusted with cruddy muddy-colored oil. There was a squawk near my feet, and I saw another yellow beak sticking out of an orange crate. I moved out of its range.

"Right. They've a vicious peck when they're scared. Why don't you stand over here by the cornmeal bath and be ready to take over. Slow and easy does it. And don't let him get that nip—I've seen them take off a fingertip, and they'll make for the eye, too."

Allan apparently didn't notice that I hadn't agreed to help. With a sigh I moved to the other sink. Allan's sink was filled with mineral oil and mine had cornmeal. The idea was that he would bathe the bird, I would cover it in cornmeal, wrap it in a towel and hand it back. He would clean it all off and then, if it still sprouted oil, he'd give it another bath.

I could feel disaster rising in me as I watched Allan confidently dip the pecking grebe in the mineral oil, and gently stroke its wings and underfeathers. Its long neck kept striking out like a snake. But Allan was deft, and it pecked at air and gradually stopped trying to flap its wings, holding its swan-like head still, stiff and anxious.

"Ready?" Allan asked, grinning.

I must have nodded, because he set the dripping oily grebe in the cornmeal before me. The bird wiggled down into the golden grain and stared up at me, daring me, his beady eyes blaming me for everything; oil slick, the indignity of the bath, the loss of his freedom. He hated me. And there was Allan watching. I could tell it was going to be worse than dropping the typewriter. It would be a first date to amuse my grandchildren, no doubt about that!

"O.K. bird—take it easy," I whispered and dug into the gritty yellow meal. Gingerly I sprinkled some on his wings and over his back. He arched his neck, and I drew back. Neither of us moved for a long moment, until finally I reached in again and dumped a handful over him and started to smooth cornmeal off the wings and rub it into the pinfeathers as I'd seen Allan do with the oil, careful always to keep my head out of the way of that malevolent beak. The bird stayed still. Maybe I'd put it into shock?

I looked over at Allan, but he was totally involved in cleaning the other grebe. He seemed not to care that he'd trusted his bird to a girl who had never held a bird in her life and dropped typewriters besides. He trusted me.

The feathers were softer than the underbelly of a cat, and the whole bird was delicately beautiful. He curved his long neck, like a miniature black swan. How vulnerable he must feel with us and yet he did seem trusting. I began to enjoy stroking cornmeal over him. We would send him back to his ocean clean and free. Maybe Allan and I were the only humans who would ever touch him, and he'd given us his trust.

Ever so gently I wiped some oil from around his eyes. He squawked and jerked his head but did not strike out at me. I smoothed cornmeal in under the wings where the feathers were softest and deepest. The oily water line must hit the grebes at just that spot. I was glad my fingernails were short so I couldn't stab him accidentally.

"Hey, you're smiling," Allan said. "Good work. That should be enough. I'll trade you."

Trade me? We'd lose both birds. We'd both get our eyes pecked out. He was out of his mind. Did he think he was talking to a trained surgical nurse? No, no, no, I kept thinking as Allan picked up my bird.

"Take my bird and put him in the cornmeal," Allan commanded and, without stopping to think, I did just what he said. I carried a strange bird, and I didn't get bitten. I did, however, get mineral oil down the front of my Levis and shirt.

Allan was examining the bird I'd washed in corn-meal. Carefully he brushed cornmeal off wings and front and underbelly.

"Think he could stand another run-through," he decided, and gently returned the grebe to the mineral oil.

That time I went right to work; cautiously, for I knew I could still lose an eye or a finger if I unwittingly frightened the bird.

"This may be a big waste of time, you know. They may die anyway, no matter what we do. It's the shock," Allan said later when he was showing me through the cages of gulls, grebes, sandpipers, and other birds I couldn't recognize and was ashamed to ask about.

"I just loved it, bathing those grebes. I just loved it," I blurted out.

"Would you like to come sometime when I go beachcombing, looking for birds?"

"Oh, yes." I would have gone off to Australia. But there was that word again—sometime. Why didn't he ever name a day, an hour, and a place? It was just my luck to fall for a sometime kind of guy.

8

ALLAN DIDN'T REMAIN A SOMETIME KIND OF GUY. As soon as I got home on Sunday he phoned and invited me to the beach after school the next day. I was waiting out in front so he wouldn't see the messy house.

The big box in back of the pickup housed a brown pelican. "Brown pelicans are still migrating, and I've got to get this guy back so he can leave or at least give him a chance to go with his own kind. I just called you because it seemed like you might be interested."

"Oh, I am." Did he have to make so absolutely certain I realized this wasn't a date? Maybe *he* ought to try going with his own kind, like me, for example, instead of concentrating on the pelicans of the world. However, he had called me, and that was something.

We got to the beach about sunset. There was no kaleidoscope of color, just an orange ball dropping from a blue sky behind a pale grey ocean, a winter ocean. The minus tide was placid, curling onto the beach. Far down the beach the lighthouse at Point Reyes blew its fog horn, but the fog bank wouldn't reach our beach for an hour or so. Flocks of seagulls rose briefly, screeching at the pickup as we slowly cruised through them, dropping back to the warm sand and folding their wings again as soon as we passed. Sandpipers scurried out of our way. Allan said the sandpipers reminded him of dune buggies because they pitched forward as if someone had put oversized tires on their rear ends.

Two or three miles down the beach Allan noticed a flock of pelicans diving just past the first breakers. He pulled the pickup to a stop.

"See them? Must be after a school of perch," he said.

He slid the box off the tailgate of the truck and set it on the sand. Then he opened the door and stood back. The pelican tested his wings, found they hit against the sides of his prison, and sat back down. It must have been a full five minutes before that bird got up again and poked his head outside. Gradually he moved out, stepping through sand that seemed to annoy him, and testing his wings as he walked toward the water. He stood in the foam at the water's edge and when a new breaker rolled lazily in, that spoiled pelican finally stretched his wings and flew, rose on a draft, and circled out to sea.

"Let's go," Allan said, starting the car.

"Don't you want to see if he goes to the others?"

"No, he's on his own."

I was soon to learn that Allan had seen one bird he'd cared for and released killed by an angry flock, and he didn't want to risk seeing anything like that again.

After that one day at the beach, I went through a time when nothing except Allan and birds mattered at all. I haunted the library. My days were calendared by the migrating birds I might find along our beach or back on the sand dunes. And I trailed Allan like a shadow. He tolerated me the way Crusoe must have put up with Friday. And he never asked me out at night, even to watch the owls, so we were no help to Dolly and Chris Roberts. He said he couldn't get "involved" with any girl.

Since I remained as determined as ever to keep Allan away from our house, it also meant I was seldom at home myself.

Then one day in April, my mother's birthday, I walked into the house to find Miss Susan Morgan, our social worker, pacing the floor. I hadn't seen her since the three old women had turned off the gas, and I hadn't missed her either.

It had been a sunny day, after a week of wind and rain, and I'd stopped to pick a few poppies and lupines. The lupines were just coming out, and I'd had to hunt for enough blooming flowers to make the bouquet. Ordinarily, I didn't approve of picking wild flowers because there were already too many people and too few flowers in our part of California; but Mom had a lousy cold, and I knew it would cheer her up to see that the lupines and poppies were out already. Winter was over, and she could be out in the sun soon. The flowers would spell out again all the reasons she had named me after her birthday month. Besides, I had no money to get Mom a bought present.

"Does it always take you this long to get home?" Miss Morgan asked. I ignored her and walked to the bed where Mom lay coughing.

"Happy birthday. How do you feel?" I asked, handing her the flowers. She smiled but shook her head. The poppies and lupines lay in her open hand. It looked as if she tried to close the fingers around the flowers but just couldn't, so I took one poppy and one lupine and held them close for her to see. She smiled and nodded. Her hand felt terribly hot.

"There was no fire when I came. It was freezing cold in here," Miss Morgan growled.

"You keep telling me, go to school, go to school." I started yelling, but I could see Mom wince, so I shut up. Apparently the social worker had lit the fire, because it seemed warm enough to me. I could see the flames reflected on Mom's exhausted face, yellow and blue flickering over the drawn still nose and mouth.

72

Only the closed eyes twitched occasionally, as if she had twinges of pain. Her face showed the same patient suffering as those of martyrs in history book pictures, which I had never believed. I turned away.

"I've called an ambulance," Miss Morgan whispered.

"So good," Mom murmured.

"To go to the hospital? But she only has a cold!" I was yelling again.

"Her temperature is 104 degrees. I think she must have pneumonia," Miss Morgan whispered, pulling me over to the other side of the room. Her hands were shaking, and her fingers kept pulling little fuzz balls from my sweater. I noticed that she had the same long fingers that my mother had, except that Miss Morgan wore natural polish on her nails and had no nicotine stains.

"Stop whispering like a whistle. Fermine can probably hear you next door." I backed out of reach of those grasping fingers.

"Sorry, April, but I've been here all alone for two hours—waiting for the ambulance. I've never seen pneumonia, and I don't know what to do for her. Maybe I should have asked the man next door to drive, but his car is open, so cold, and I thought the ambulance would be here hours ago."

"But it was only a bad cold this morning," I said, and wished I'd checked her temperature.

"These things turn suddenly. You just never know.

But I don't even know if she's in a crisis. Have you ever seen one? Oh, why don't they come, why don't they *come?*" She started toward my sweater; I backed away, and she stood twisting her hands. Her grey eyes were wide, and I covered my own against their fright.

"I'm so afraid she's going to——"

"No, she's not," I said harshly.

Miss Morgan sat down in the rocking chair and began to sob quietly. Her long blond hair fell across her face. I thought she was like a cat meowing.

Mom was sleeping. Her mouth hung open and her breath came in rasping gulps. I found myself listening for each one, annoyed with Miss Morgan because her crying made it more difficult to hear. I had seen a movie once where a woman who breathed like that was in a coma. What did you do to bring someone out of a coma? Mom always said my strong hobo coffee would bring back the dead. It was worth a try.

"Mom, do you want me to make a cup of coffee?"

There was no answer, no sound in the room but Miss Morgan sobbing and the gulping struggle for each breath. It was hard to believe she'd gotten so sick without my knowing. I didn't know what to do, and Miss Morgan was twice my age and being paid to help and there she was rocking away feeling sorry for herself. It wasn't as if she were crying over Mom. She was wailing because the ambulance hadn't come, and if anything happened she was afraid she'd be blamed. She wasn't helping Mom, especially since my mother believed the vibrations in a place determined how you felt. When I thought of it, I realized Mom hadn't started gasping until Miss Morgan started sobbing. I could see she was getting hysterical. Somehow I *had* to stop her. I stood over her rocking chair. All I could see was her long blond hair and hunched body. Suddenly I grabbed a wad of that hair and pulled Miss Morgan's head straight back. Her face was red and blotchy and startled.

"Cut that out! Can't you hear how my mother *is* since you started? You're making her worse. Please— I'm sorry—but please stop." I let go and was horrified to see that I had a handful of hair.

Miss Morgan stared at me—then at the hair in my hand—then at my mother—then back to me, and I could see the anger draining out of her face. She went to the bed and took Mom's hand, counting the pulse, I suppose. She sighed, patted the hand, and pulled a chair up to the bed. I took her still warm place in the rocking chair. We did not speak.

I do not know how long we waited, listening to Mom's breathing and watching the fire in the gathering darkness. Twice I put wood on the fire. I wondered about turning on the lights, but I did not want to see Miss Morgan's face and so I delayed. I wondered if Mom had any aspirin, if she ought to take some, and if I should get Fermine. I knew I should bring Fermine, but I did not move. I could not.

Finally a car stopped outside, crunching gravel.

Was it the ambulance? I heard no siren. Doors slammed; they sounded like gunshots in the still night. Even my mother twitched in her restless sleep.

"This the place? There's no numbers, and there's no lights on in there. Want to give it a try?"

Miss Morgan jumped up and ran through the front door, waving her scarf at the sound of the man's voice.

"Here, here. Thank God you've come," she called.

I turned on the lights. My chair was still rocking when she came back with two enormous young men carrying a stretcher between them. Both men wore white. The man at the rear balanced the stretcher on the end of the bed while the one with the stethoscope around his neck took hold of my mother's wrist. She opened her eyes and smiled at him.

"I'm Dr. Thompson, ma'am. We're going to take you on to the hospital with us. You'll be a lot more comfortable there. How long you been feeling poorly?"

My mother shook her head and closed her eyes, still smiling. The doctor listened to her chest with the stethoscope. I waited until he was done and then waited again while he felt along her arms and legs.

"She only seemed to have a cold this morning," I said.

"It's all right," he answered, looking straight at me.

Just then there was a loud knock on the door.

I opened it to find Fermine holding a birthday cake covered with lighted candles.

"Happy birthday to you, Happy birth-day—to—you——Jesus, Mary, Mother of God, what happen? Who are these men? The stretcher. I see the lights so I think to celebrate the birthday. What happen, April, what happen to your mother? May the blessed Saints protect you, Mary, for the good woman you are."

We all stood there while Fermine, still carrying the lighted birthday cake, advanced toward the bed. I had the crazy feeling he was going to ask her to blow out the candles. They were burning down in thirty-five blobs of red wax and melting the whipping cream, something Fermine never let happen. He stood looking down at her, and the expression in the old man's eyes was so tender I felt embarrassed. I remembered Fermine looking at me that way once when I'd broken my arm.

"She won't die?" he asked the man with the stretcher.

"Ah, no, Fermine. Not now, when winter is over," my mother whispered.

"She'll be just fine, sir."

"The cake is whole wheat and real cream, all good for her," Fermine said gently.

I almost had to laugh when my mother turned her head away. I knew how she dreaded Fermine's cakes.

"Later, later," the doctor said more abruptly, moving in front of Fermine. He folded back the blankets and, setting the stretcher alongside Mom, the two men lifted her very gently onto the taut white canvas. She was skin and bones. Then the ambulance attendant stretched a grey blanket over her. Miss Morgan opened the door.

"Can I go with you? I want to be with her," I said as they lifted my mother.

Mom nodded her head, her eyes still closed.

"I'm her daughter. Tell them she needs me, Fermine!"

The man with the stethoscope, the doctor, seemed to consider.

"Please, she'll be worried if I'm not there. She really will."

"Get your coat and make it snappy, then, little lady. Who phoned? We'll need someone to check this woman in. A responsible adult—follow in your own car, please."

"Yes, I will. April, get your coat," Miss Morgan said as the stretcher passed her, and the men carried my mother out into the night.

For a moment I just stood still. I saw Fermine blow out the candles and set the cake on the table. I could hear him saying Hail Marys under his breath. Mom was Catholic, too, so that would probably help.

Miss Morgan helped me into my coat and gave me a little push. I turned to Fermine.

"That was nice about the cake," I said.

"She will not be able to eat it," he answered sadly.

"I will. Keep on saying them, the prayers," I mumbled and ran out the door. I had to hurry, or they'd leave me behind. I could hear the gravel crunching and the ambulance door opening. But at the top of the driveway I turned and looked back down the dark path into the lighted room. I was glad to see Fermine sitting by the fire in the rocking chair. It would be easier to come home, knowing someone was there.

Gingerly I stepped up and into the ambulance. I sat on a long bench alongside my mother's stretcher. The young doctor sat next to me, taking her pulse. The other man slammed the door shut. I had braced myself for blackness, but there was a small light. I could see that my mother was sleeping peacefully on the stretcher, her breathing almost normal.

The siren started, low and moaning, stridently cutting into the night. I knew all our neighbors would be rushing out to see what was going on. Everyone in town would be watching us, wondering who was dying, who had to be rushed to the hospital, wondering if we'd make it in time. Only it wasn't true. It wasn't true! The doctor *said* she'd be just fine. I wished I'd brought some Kleenex.

9

As it happened i had to ask Fermine to turn out the lights in our house because I stayed on in San Luis with Susan Morgan. Mom became delirious and remained so most of the week. I stayed until Miss Morgan became Sue and her blue velvet fold-out bed became home.

I got used to the delirium. Mom tossed and muttered, talking about *her* mother. Couldn't she wait until it got warm to wash down the front steps? Or until she'd practiced her violin cantata before she waxed the hall steps? Or until she'd finished the chapter she was reading before cleaning the bathroom? She pricked her fingers embroidering, no wonder since she was so nearsighted, and asked if she couldn't leave it until the fingers healed. And often, she apologized for burning the pancakes she was making for her brothers. She was afraid of turning them because she'd flipped a pancake clear onto the floor.

She became very quiet when she came out of the delirium. She'd lie staring at the ceiling, or sleeping. If she was that way, I'd turn around and go back to Susan's. Still, I didn't think of leaving town. Allan and Dolly and Fermine and school belonged to another life. They were good to think about, but nothing to make me leave Mom. Fermine was the only person I really missed.

I liked to be near, but I hated visiting the hospital after a while. She was in a six-bed ward, and the other five ladies had nothing in the world to do but stare at me from the minute I walked in until I left. I sweated under their scrutiny no matter what deodorant I used.

One night I pushed through the heavy swinging door into her ward. The big electric clock over the elevator read seven-thirty. Visiting hours were over by eight and that would be time enough. Maybe some of the women were asleep. I hoped I wouldn't be the only visitor.

Mom lay in a starched white hospital gown on a high white bed. It was as if she were buried in a snowdrift up to her neck so that only her head and those long reaching arms were alive, as if the rest had been amputated or maybe only paralyzed. She was staring at the ceiling.

I stood by the door deciding whether I could leave or had to try to say hello. The other women watched me to see what I would do. Then I saw that they weren't the only ones. A young man in white sat in the chair next to her bed. He sat with his legs crossed and his chair tilted back into the shadow of the curtain; his arms hugged his chest as if he'd been there a long while and was resting. I started to back quietly out the door.

"Don't go away, April. Aren't you April?" the man asked. He was blond and had an old man's sad smile on his young face.

I crossed the tile floor. My crepe soles made the only sound in the room as they caught on the tile squares.

"Don't be afraid. I've heard your mother say you're a fine girl. I'm Dr. Owen. Has she mentioned me?"

I nodded, trying to remember what Mom had said about him besides that he was the young one. I could see that.

"Has this ever happened before? The withdrawal, I mean. Does your mother—has she had a shock of any kind that you remember?"

"She's had pneumonia. She's tired." I heard one of the women snicker as I spoke. Roughly, I reached over and shook Mom.

"It's me, Mom. Listen, you've got to hear me. Please, Mom!" I kept shaking her, aware that the doctor was watching me.

"Sometimes it helps to take both hands and pull her

up a little." The woman in the next bed rolled toward us, hauling about 200 pounds after her. "Mary, Mary, you have company."

The doctor was leaning forward in his chair as I shook her, but I couldn't help it. She had to wake up and keep him from asking me any more questions.

"Is that how you wake her at home, April?" he asked, very softly. He sounded like someone else; he sounded like Susan that time she got me talking about the night walks and was going to send me to a foster home. I wasn't going to get caught in that routine again.

"She's had pneumonia," I said again. There was such a lump in my throat I sounded raspy.

"Hi, Mom."

"Hello, there," the doctor shouted as if she were hard of hearing.

"Is it morning yet?" Mom asked, reaching for my hand. Hers was still hot.

"Nope, not even lights out yet, Mary," the fat woman said. The doctor frowned at her, and she turned over.

"Mrs. MacLeash has a daughter, too, April, but older. With two children of her own already. She doesn't look old enough, does she, doctor?" My mother's hand was groping on the night table for her cigarettes. I handed them to her with some matches. She lit one, inhaling with satisfaction, as she glanced brightly from one of us to the other. My mother al-

ways expected all her acquaintances to like one another.

"I'm glad to see you so much better," the doctor
said, smiling broadly. "I'd like to see you cut down on
those cigarettes, though." He patted her hand profes-
sionally.

"Ah, I know. Well, it will be easier at home, and
that won't be long now, will it, Dr. Owen?" There
was a worried question in my mother's voice. She kept
trying to catch the doctor's eye, but he took her pulse
and kept his eyes on his watch.

"Not too long, now," he said, patting her on the
shoulder and turning to go. "I'll see you again, young
lady. I'd like to have a talk with you."

I didn't like the way Mom looked after him, as if
she were frightened. I had wanted to ask him when
she was going home, but I couldn't. Then he would
stay and ask more questions. Besides, her main doctor,
the one who would tell me, was only there in the
morning. I wondered if he and this doctor talked.

As soon as the swinging door closed, I spoke, sur-
prising myself. "Mom, I want to go home and wait
there. I should be in school."

"Yes, the rain has stopped now."

It took me a moment to figure out she was saying
yes, I could go, because the leaking roof wouldn't give
me pneumonia as it had her. The rain had stopped.

Mrs. MacLeash whined, "If you go home, will you
be able to come and see your mother while she's here?"

"It doesn't matter. I'll be home soon," Mom said. "We need visitors."

"Maybe Fermine could bring me. But you'll be home by next week, won't you?"

"You never know," Mrs. MacLeash stated ominously. I gave her a dirty look, and she shut up, pursing her lips. I wanted to fix her with the evil eye so she'd grunt and roll back over.

"My temperature's almost down—only a hundred now. They need the beds, so they won't keep me much longer?"

That question in my mother's voice again. What was she so worried about—it must be either her temperature or those doctors with the soft voices of snakes who kept asking questions. They were creepy, all right.

"You should bring your mother flowers. It makes the nurses nicer if they think somebody cares." Mrs. MacLeash joined us again.

"Ah, don't worry about me," my mother said, reaching for my hand. I circumvented this by pouring a glass of water and drinking it; that hot clammy hand bothered me, like one of us was dead.

"Other hospitals, they bring you juice at night. Or maybe even cocoa," Mrs. MacLeash said.

I turned my back on her and spoke quietly. "Susan's gotten us a stove with an automatic pilot. Maybe Fermine can get it hooked up by the time you're back. I'll bet the poppies are all out with this hot weather."

"I wonder how many bottles the milkman has left by the kitchen door," Mom said, and we both laughed.

It was a good time to leave. I bent over quickly and kissed Mom on the forehead. It felt warm but dry. I brushed back her hair. It was a relief to find how thick it still was.

"It's better for you to be in school," Mom said sadly.

"I'm going to run before they throw me out. I'll be back, take care," and I fled.

I pushed blindly through the swinging door of the room. There had been tears in my mother's eyes. There were tears in mine as I looked around carefully to avoid running into that doctor.

"She could have stayed another ten minutes. She left early." Mrs. MacLeash's voice echoed after me and into the long hall. My crepe soles caught on the asphalt tile, holding back my departure step by step.

"Surely you can see I couldn't let them talk to me?" I asked, but, of course, there was no answer.

10

I ARRIVED HOME AFTER MIDNIGHT AND, AS I CLOSED
the door behind me, I knew the house was finally my
own. Susan, who had been terribly hard to convince,
drifted away with the distant backfire of her little
sports car. The moon silhouetted the beds and tables
and dressers that were a part of my home. I could live
my own life there, and it would be nobody's business
but my own. I would be, no, I *was* free.

I could hear the wind coming in from the ocean and
far off the low mournful cry of the fog horn. The
eucalyptus sighed and cracked with the wind, sending
a tang of cough drops filtering through the house. I
built a fire, and pulled my bed close to its warmth.

Tomorrow, after school, I decided I would tear into

the place and give it the cleaning of its life. And stock the refrigerator. And invite Allan and Dolly over. And maybe Fermine would haul a load of old milk bottles to the dump.

The next thing I remember was a terrible pounding. I rubbed my eyes and tried to force them open. Daylight. I'd be late for school. Someone was knocking on the back door. I stumbled out of bed, my bare feet patting the freezing linoleum as I went to see who it was.

"Breakfast time, April." Fermine stood smiling at the back door.

"You can smile. You've probably been up for hours," I growled. "How did you know I was even home?"

"Your social worker called me."

"And she went on for hours about how she trusts me—like a hole in the head! All right, all right! Five minutes." I tried to close the door, but Fermine leaned around me and peered inside.

"That bed so close to the fire. You might get burned. Move it back."

"I'll sleep wherever I please. Let me alone, Fermine. Now, I mean it!"

He whipped by me and sent the cot screeching across the floor in one movement, without effort, like a lion slapping his cub. There was no anger in his face, just a terrible smugness. He'd done something like that before. I was about six and trying to help him weed. I'd accidentally pulled something he wanted. Without a word he'd lifted me by the seat of the pants and thrown me over the fence. I could still taste dirt in my mouth and feel the wrenching pain of the twisted ankle I'd landed on. And remember my tears. Well, I wasn't crying for his majesty again.

"This is my house. Not yours. You are nothing but a nosy old man! Now get out and stay out!"

"Breakfast in five minutes," he said quietly, and closed the door behind him.

"Eat it yourself. I'll *never*, never eat with you again!"

Ten minutes later Fermine was waiting by his back gate. He handed me a small flat package wrapped in aluminum foil. I knew there would be fresh tortillas and cheese, chilies and some April surprise inside. I took the package, nodded, and walked on, warming my hands on the aluminum foil. I noticed that the joints on Fermine's hand were swollen with arthritis, but I did not ask about the pain.

Because, if I moved the bed near a fire again, he would shove it back across the floor no matter how swollen his hands. My privacy meant nothing. My decisions meant less. In fact, the breakfast was only another proof that he was boss. He said he'd make me breakfast and he had. Granted that he was right about the bed being too close to the fire, did that give him the right to make me bow down on everything? He was only the next-door neighbor, after all.

I held the warm package against my cheek. How

delicious tortillas and cheese smelled in the early morning! My stomach churned, waiting. And didn't Fermine know it, too?

I took aim and threw the steaming package against the trunk of a pine just as hard as I could. The foil burst and food spattered over the grass and sand for a 5-foot radius. Tomatoes and lettuce, the first of the season. That must have been the surprise. A piece of tortilla stuck to the tree trunk and, picking my way through the wreckage of my breakfast, I lifted it off and ate it.

"I just wish you could know. Oh, I'd love to see your false teeth drop out if you knew!" My voice was harsh in the still air. Then, as the sound died away, I remembered Fermine looking down at Mom when they took her to the hospital and, before that, at me when I was hurt. I couldn't get rid of those loving gentle eyes.

I didn't stop running until I reached school. My school looked bare and small and run down after the county hospital. Strange that I'd never noticed what a shabby old dump it was. I scanned the playground and spotted Dolly playing volleyball. Everyone else on the court was running about lunging for the ball while Dolly leisurely raised the inside of her wrist and flipped it over the net. I saw Chris Roberts flip it back. Dolly returned, and so did Chris. They were playing each other and the rest of the kids might as well have been in China for all the good their exercise was doing the game. Dolly missed, and I saw her face flush. She was mad. Dolly always said you should let the boys win, but she didn't look too happy with Chris's victory. Very interesting!

"Hi, April. Happy day after Easter."

It was Allan, and he held out a chocolate bunny that must have been a foot tall.

"Know the definition of a pessimist?" he asked, gently laying the bunny in my hands. "A pessimist is someone who's afraid of the Easter bunny because he may have rabies."

"I'll put him in quarantine." I laughed. He laughed with me, reaching over and taking my free hand and holding on. This was a rare gesture for Allan, who generally treated me like a little brother. I longed to know if it was because he missed me or in sympathy but could not ask. There was a warmth in the way he was looking at me that made it difficult to keep my balance.

"Hello, love birds," Dolly called from halfway across the playground.

Allan dropped my hand as if he had been burned and moved a step or two away from me. He shrugged, and I returned the shrug before Dolly bore down on us.

"Wow! Am I glad you're back. I gained 3 pounds from sheer boredom this last week. How's your Mom? Is she home?"

"She's better, but she's staying a few days, just in

case. I have the house to myself until she gets back," I said as soon as Dolly paused for breath.

"Is it lonely?" Allan asked gently.

"I remember when I stayed alone. I was in consumate ecstasies—until—I don't know how I got started on that. Fool that I am, *of course it's great!* Freedom. Privacy. Eureka, the house is mine," Dolly called out, hugging her hands to her chest and casting her eyes to the sky.

Allan lifted that left eyebrow. We both knew it must have been the time Dolly's parents went off for a drive and didn't come back because of that "totally useless accident."

"Why not come on over and see how it is?" I asked as casually as I could manage. "How about tomorrow?"

The bell rang. Allan nodded, tugged at the ear of the bunny he'd given me, and ran for class.

"Lord have mercy," Dolly laughed, "you couldn't keep me away."

As it turned out, they couldn't come until Thursday because Allan had to work on the farm, which was a blessing. It gave me two extra days to work on operation House Beautiful.

Fermine, who was delighted to fix the house for Mom, helped. We washed, waxed, and repaired everything in sight and then painted the kitchen for good measure. Painting is the most satisfying housework of all because it makes such a change with so little effort.

Of course, I *did* hate to ask Fermine for help, but since I didn't know how to fix collapsing chairs or wax floors, for example, there wasn't much choice.

"And the sad truth is that Mom will probably never notice our efforts," I growled sometime after midnight Wednesday.

"The kitchen was blue and now it is yellow," Fermine suggested.

"And God knows the place reeks of fresh paint," I mourned.

"You will have to put her bed again where she can see the sunrise. She likes to celebrate the morning."

"Oh, I will, but I have two friends coming tomorrow," I said.

Fermine's eyes narrowed. "Who gave the permission?"

"They are only coming for an hour in the afternoon. Since when can't I even have someone visit me? Other girls can have friends over anytime they want, but—I only have tomorrow, Fermine. Please?"

I knew it was no time to fight with Fermine. If he got stubborn, it could be fatal. There was no way to guess what he was thinking. In despair I decided I should never have asked his help.

"Boy?" he asked.

"One boy and one girl." Bless Dolly, bless her soul.

"We cleaned up for the boy and girl?" he asked wryly. "Don't. I don't want you to have to lie for me. I'll make you some cookies tomorrow," he said finally.

I sank down into the rocking chair. Another crisis passed. Fermine's cookies were the world's worst, but Allan would eat anything and Dolly was dieting.

What the house really looked like, I decided after Fermine was gone and I was alone with the sense of it, was a nice old lady's house. One who was still interested in life, so she had books and pictures and flowers around. That was undoubtedly how Allan would expect my mother's house to look. The image fit.

Then why was I still uneasy? Why did I jump when the owls hooted from the eucalyptus trees and tremble when the coyotes howled on the mesa, miles away?

II

I WAS STILL APPREHENSIVE THE NEXT AFTERNOON AS I looked over the house for the last time. There must be something missing, something I'd forgotten, though I'd checked the list a dozen times. Certainly there were too many flowers. They made the room look as if it existed only to be photographed, and I picked up a crowded bowl of iris to set outside.

The phone rang. Every instinct said I should not answer, and yet something about the repeated ringing worked its way into my spinal cord, jarring me enough to pick up the receiver.

There was no mistaking the voice on the other end of the line. That high nasal whine could belong to no one but our sheriff, Gopher Grodin. And no one else called me "April girl."

"Oh, no! Maybe she's just in the bathroom." She'd probably gone, taken a walk, but why let him know I thought so? Why couldn't Mom have waited just a couple of hours, only until Dolly and Allan had gone? That one afternoon. Oh, stop wailing, April. After all, the really important thing is did she bother to dress first or is she out flapping around in nothing but a hospital gown?

"Isn't she free to leave when she wants? She's not in jail, you know," I said witheringly. Of course I knew pneumonia patients didn't normally walk away, but was there a law against it? Maybe—or why would they call Gopher Grodin? The hospital was fifteen miles away.

"I'm sure the hospital would be glad to know you go around threatening to put ladies with pneumonia in your mildewing old jail. No, I don't want you to come by for me. I happen to be busy this afternoon. If she comes in, I'll let you know. Mom's old enough to take care of herself," I said. His voice was not only high-pitched but a monotone, so that it was hard to catch. Was he actually talking about catching her and bringing her back *for* me? Maybe they had the whole police department out rounding her up like a maverick steer. I began to feel sick to my stomach and couldn't think of anything nasty enough to say, which gave him time to pretend he felt like my big brother. If anything, I would have asked him about the abalone shell NO I'd

96

left on his front lawn. He started saying I shouldn't be mad because it wasn't his fault, he didn't have anything to do with Mom running away.

"She *didn't* run away. She probably went out for a pack of cigarettes and a decent cup of coffee," I said, but then I started crying so I set down the phone. I stared at the bowl of iris still in my other hand; blurred by tears, they looked better. It was crazy to throw away fresh flowers, so I set them in front of the phone; then, reaching over them, I took the receiver off the hook.

What next? I was trying to decide if she might have put a coat over the backless white hospital gown and where she might be when I heard Dolly and Allan coming down our gravel path. Dolly's high laugh hung in the silence like the ring of the phone.

They knocked. Dolly's face filled the glass squares in the top of the door as if she were peering out from behind bars. We looked at each other. I couldn't move from the rocking chair. If Mom had nothing on but that hospital gown, we were in real trouble. If she stayed out after it got cold or dark, we were also in for it.

The door scraped as Dolly pushed it open. She and Allan were there for tea. Ready or not.

"Oh, you just know your mama has to be a poet. I can just feel it. This house is the reincarnation of Wordsworth's cottage." Dolly went around the room, touching books and pictures, and I could see how it must be for her. Out at her place they had the Bible on the mantel, but that was the only book I remembered seeing outside of Dolly's room. "Don't worry, April, I really know houses don't have reincarnations. Don't let me say stupid things like that."

"It's kind of a mess," I said.

"What's wrong, April?" Allan asked quietly.

Dolly swung round then and looked at me, really saw me for the first time. "She's had a relapse," she groaned.

"No, she's gone, walked out of the hospital, and they've got old Gopher Grodin tracking her down." I felt dizzy and there were stars going around and then the next thing I remember, I was lying on the bed. Allan was holding my hand, and Dolly was banging dishes. I got cramped with him holding my hand and shoved my arms under the blanket. I didn't like him feeling sorry for me.

"Dolly's making tea," he said.

"And my wing's not even broken."

Allan grinned. He understood. "I thought maybe you flew into a window. Seriously, I've got the pickup. Why don't I go look for her. She'd rather see me than Gopher."

"Who wouldn't? Even *I* would rather see you than Gopher Grodin." Dolly laughed nervously.

I lay on the bed and listened to Dolly and Allan, and it was clear that they'd heard something about Mom. They were jittery and didn't ask questions like *why* she'd taken off or *why* the sheriff had the posse out, which was what I wanted to know. However, I didn't care anymore. It wasn't any use. In a way, whatever they knew made it easier because I wouldn't have known how to explain. I could just lie there and look up at the ceiling where the spiders still lived. With all the cleaning, Fermine and I hadn't thought to sweep down one cobweb. That was typical.

"The thing is," I began wearily, "that I shouldn't have come home. And I wouldn't have, except that the doctors kept asking her questions all the time, and they wanted to have heart-to-heart talks with me, too; and the last heart-to-heart talk I had nearly landed me in a foster home. I guess the problem is that they want her to be like them, so they'll be happier, and no one seems to care that Mom and I both like things the way they are. They can't let us alone."

"Who?" Dolly asked.

"What do you mean who?"

"Who can't let you alone?"

"Everyone. Social workers, doctors, everyone. That's a stupid question."

"But why *you*—your mother's a grown woman. She can take care of herself. Who made you her watchdog? Now, April, don't get your dander up. I only mean that you can go find her now, but you can't run her life for her—any more than I can stop my little old grandmother from wasting eighty years behind a dustcloth."

99

"You do not understand—I'm not trying——"

"Let's go. It'll be dark in a couple of hours. If we're going——"Allan had been standing by the window with his back to us, and as he talked he shrugged into his jacket. "Can't you two talk some other time," he added with obvious annoyance.

"How about the tea?"

"Later, Doll, later. Here's your sweater. April?"

I nodded and reached out a hand to each of them. We held on tight for a moment. I was still mad at Dolly, but holding on helped.

"Where shall we start?" Allan asked, clearing his throat and dropping our hands.

12

THE LATE AFTERNOON SUN STILL HUNG COMFORTABLY over the valley and it would be another hour before the poppies closed. A gusty warm wind blew against the pickup as we drove up the highway toward San Luis. We kept to the right lane, creeping along so we wouldn't miss her. I sat between Allan and Dolly in the truck cab, hunched forward to watch both sides of the road. Allan's arm lay around my shoulder and his hand kneeded me gently, as if he were easing a sore muscle. Dolly snapped on the radio and hummed along with the singer. The song was about traveling on and I could almost be lulled into believing we were.

"I wouldn't even know her if we did see her," Dolly said into the silence after the number ended.

"Just tell us if you see *anybody*. Look, cedar wax-
wings. So many this year, and they've been around
so long. Usually a week and they travel on. Over in
the clump of willows on the left, April." Allan nodded
toward a flurry of small tawny birds; rising in a cloud,
they hovered like bees, circled, and settled back into
the same willow patch by the side of the road.

"Where are they usually this time of year?" I
asked.

"Should be in Portland eating bugs off the roses
by April," he called over the radio commercial.

We passed three hitchhikers about our age and
signaled that we were only going a short distance.
They smiled, and one of them waved.

I wondered if one of us should have stayed home,
just to be in touch with the hospital. It was anybody's
guess whether she'd even stay along the highway. It
might be another wild goose chase, but we were into
it now and if we could save Mom from having Gopher
Grodin pull up behind her, sirens full blast, I'd comb
every road in the county.

We had been hunting about an hour. First, we'd
covered San Luis street by street, and then we began
backtracking the highway, tracing the route she might
have taken if she had started home. About four miles
out of San Luis, Dolly started in about religion.

"What I mean is what religion *was* she—when she
was a tyke? Well—Allan, in times of trouble people
do revert and this area is full of churches."

102

"She's still a Catholic, more or less. I mean, she still goes to Mass sometimes. I don't know, I've never thought to look in a church but I've never found her either." For the first time in a year I wanted to bite my nails, but that would really turn Allan off, so I pressed my hands between my knees and tried to think about churches.

"The Mission, if any place," Allan said, and we went back to the Mission. The priests looked us over but no one said anything. She wasn't there.

It was a relief to be back on the highway. I knew Allan was beginning to think about getting home for milking his cows. I thought I ought to phone the hospital.

"Look at that cunning church," Dolly said hesitantly.

We were passing an old chapel set back in a little grove of weeping willow trees. It looked peculiarly deserted and weather-beaten against the vivid green of the leafing trees. The building tilted so that the steeple leaned into the willows and only the wooden cross rose out of the lush green. The church must have been white once, but had long since taken on the grey-brown of all neglected wood.

"She *is* Catholic and that *is* just the kind of place she loves—a building you don't have to live up to, she calls it."

I felt guilty when Allan made a *U* turn and headed back toward the deserted church. I could see he thought it was a useless bore, and I knew he was most likely right. I'd never found her before so why were we apt to get lucky then?

He turned off the highway onto the dirt road, spinning a cocoon of dust behind us. We stopped in a sunlit patch of weeds and lupine that must have been a parking area. Once Allan snapped off the ignition, the quiet of the place took hold. Bird song was the only sound in the gully just off the highway. I felt totally alone. It was a good spot for a church.

"I reckon she might find it down right comforting to be where God might want to come," Dolly said. "And smell that honeysuckle, will you?"

"Hmph! I thought you were a yogi," Allan snorted as he strode toward the church.

It was Allan who saw her first. She was standing in the open door with her back to us, talking to the dark interior, the filtered twilight of stained glass windows. We could see straight into the chapel to where the sun came through bullet holes. It looked as if someone had used the beautiful windows for target practice. My mother was silhouetted against the light, and I was relieved to see that she wore a bathrobe and slippers. One hand held her temple as if she had a headache or was pushing hair out of her eyes.

"She looks like a saint or a monk," Dolly whispered. "Like Joan of Arc."

"Can't you leave anything alone, Doll, anything?" Allan whispered.

We had stopped, and I knew why they whispered. My own inclination was to turn and run, to send Fermine to get her. What could *we* do? Suppose she wouldn't go back to the hospital? Maybe she'd die if we took her home. Dolly probably saw herself as the Dauphine of France or Florence Nightingale, but Allan was embarrassed, and I was scared.

"But Hitler, how about Hitler, why him—why did You make us go through him?" she asked. She'd been mumbling, but these words came through clearly.

Allan mumbled something I didn't want to hear.

Scratch one boyfriend, I thought.

"And the darkness. Soon it will be June 21 and then each day gets shorter and the forces of darkness gain," she went on.

"Mom?"

She turned slowly and looked intently right through us. We stared back at her and at the light coming through the stained glass window, and nobody moved for a long time. A wind had come up and we could hear the willow branches reluctantly sweeping the roof.

"It's me, April. Can't you see us? What happened to your glasses? Where did you leave them this time?"

She winced, possibly because she heard the anger in my voice. She dropped her eyes and turned back to what must have been the altar, although no sign of one remained, and stood, one hand on her hip, explaining to the empty church, not to us.

"Ah, the world is so much lovelier without glasses, it's the sharp edges that hurt so," she said gently. "So very much softer."

The willows brushing the roof seemed to echo our breathing. Then Allan walked over and took her arm and led her to the car. Nobody said anything. All I could think of was the day he carried my typewriter up the gravel path to Dolly's place. Dolly started to cry.

By the time we got to the car, Mom was crying, too. All the way to San Luis I kept seeing colored flashes and hoping I might faint again, but I didn't. I had my arm around her, and she looked up now and then and smiled through the tears, but I don't think she knew me.

"I can't," I said when the pickup stopped. "I can't take her back there."

So Allan took her in while Dolly and I waited.

I knew it was my place to take her back and that Allan was done with me. And it would have been better for her if I'd told the nurses I'd taken her out. But it was like taking her back to prison, and all I could do was sit in the car watching Doll cry. I couldn't even cry.

"She said it was good to get back in bed because her knees wobbled," Allan commented tersely when he came back.

He snapped on the car radio, and we drove home to the vibrating pulse of loud music. It covered our own silence. Even Doll was quiet. I'd never seen her so pre-occupied.

"My mother used to drink—just once in a blue moon—and we'd all go looking for her like this," Dolly told me, holding my hand tightly when Allan stopped at home. "Now you go take a hot bath, hear?"

"I hope she's O.K.," Allan said.

The next morning I went over to see Fermine because I could not stay alone. At Fermine's I could still hear the phone in case the hospital called. Also, though I knew Allan and I were through, there was the off chance that he just might call to see how Mom was, and I wanted to be around if he did. Fermine was whipping his string bean plants with a willow branch as I pushed through his gate.

"That's the way. Cry, cry and grow beans," he yelled at the lush vines, already five feet tall and thick with dark green leaves that lay torn and broken after his attack.

"Not again? Last year you left them alone."

"Too much rain this winter—makes them grow too well, so proud they forget to make beans. They'll be all right now. The shock will make them flower. If they think they die, then they make beans. All mother nature's creatures do the same. When there is a war, there are more babies. Look it up and you'll see."

Fermine stood back and gazed at his beaten string bean plants with satisfaction. All over the county farmers grew string beans and I had never heard of anyone else beating his beans. Fermine claimed his grandfather taught him. However it was, we had far too many string beans every summer. Fermine might have had crazy ways but his plants always grew.

"You come to help weed?" Fermine asked.

I nodded. Fermine knew something was wrong if I came to work, but he didn't ask questions. We sat in the sun weeding companionably most of the day. The phone never rang, but the sun was soothing and I felt a little better. We were about to quit when a car made a tire-burning stop out in front. I jumped up, hoping for Allan, and found Susan's sport car instead.

"Get some grape juice or something, Fermine, and please, please don't leave me alone with her," I whispered as she started down the gravel path, chewing on her chiffon scarf.

Fermine winked and disappeared into the house. I remained crouched in the tomato patch, playing for time. In a moment she'd knock on our door and I'd have to call out. I needed to feel the garden first. The thing about Fermine's garden was that it always smelled wonderful, even chives and lilac blended. And by April the fruit was set, the tomato plants were blooming, seed grapes poked down from the leafing grape arbor. There was a feeling of growing.

"O.K., over here, Susan. Fermine and I are having grape juice. How's Mom?" I asked.

"Resting. Temp's back and a nasty cough, but she'll be O.K."

Susan chain-smoked while Fermine showed her the garden; she tapped her hip while he played the guitar; and she drew little circles on the arbor table while I talked about sunset and birds.

"You know," she said finally, laying a hand on my arm, "it's going to be a while before your mother comes home."

"How long?" I'd been stalling, but it was a relief to come to the point.

"Mary?" Fermine asked, and I framed the one word "walk" silently with my lips, and he nodded and sighed.

"No one seems to know—at least a month or two. Yesterday didn't help. Never mind. *All* I'm here for is to see what we can do to help you, April, nothing else." She stubbed out her cigarette and started playing with the scarf again. She wouldn't look at me.

"Forget it. I'm fine. Come on over and see how Fermine and I fixed up the house for Mom. Maybe we'll have time to do the yard, too, and surprise her. Don't shake your head that way, Sue! All I need is a little food."

"You talk as if you were twenty-one. You have to have a guardian."

"Since when?"

We stared at each other. Susan stood up. We both knew I'd been on my own for quite a while. If she leveled with herself, she knew I'd be all right. "You're only afraid for your job," I whispered.

"It's the law, April. Whether you had me or some

other social worker, it would be the same. Minors have to have guardians, regardless."

"Mom?"

"She's not here. That's the whole point."

I looked at Susan and thought, if she cries again I will take her by the hair—no, I'll run away and never come back. I will turn and run, and when I cross the state boundary I will pull out the sign and take it with me.

"April, April, be reasonable," she pleaded.

"I *won't* go to an orphanage, and I *won't* go to a foster home, and I'll run away before you can put me in Gopher Grodin's flea house of a jail! You don't own me because I'm on welfare!" I was pounding on the table. I looked over to Fermine to show I was sorry, but he wasn't there. All I'd asked him to do was stay with me, and he'd cut out and I didn't even know when he'd gone. "Fermine! Fermine," I called.

"April, I don't want to *put* you anywhere. God knows, I think you've gone through enough already. But I can't leave you alone. It's against the law, and you'd be miserable."

The screen door slammed, and Fermine came running down the steps. His hair was flying, and his face was flushed, and in one hand he waved a parchment roll tied with a faded pink velvet ribbon. "What's all the yelling?"

"She wants——"

"I do *not!*" Susan shouted, throwing up her hands.

"Never mind. I will keep April for her mother. I found my marriage license!"

"What marriage license?" Susan and I asked in unison. Susan grabbed the roll, and we both read about Fermine's marriage forty years before to some woman whose name was no longer legible.

"Oh, I'd forgotten," I said weakly.

"We do not need to tell your bosses that my wife is dead. This is all they need," he said waving the license triumphantly.

Susan shook her head. "I only wish it *were* that simple. We could try when the juvenile authorities send your case to court, but I think they'll suggest trying to find your father."

"But I've never even met him. He wasn't even around when I was born! Fermine."

"I take good care of April."

"I'll hit the road first, and I mean it, Susan."

Fermine laid a hand on my shoulder, meaning I should calm down. "Perhaps we could write to April's father and he could say he wants her to stay with me?" he asked.

"Oh, why didn't I stay in art history?" Susan groaned. "All right, maybe it would help. At least it would buy us some time."

"Let me write. I'd kind of like to write my father."

"But do you have an extra room, Mr. Moreno?" Susan asked.

"Not for me," I said flatly. "I'm keeping our house

just like it is until Mom gets home."

"We're paying the rent," Susan said in a whisper.

"Whose side *are* you on?"

"Oh, God, *don't*, April. Let's wait and see what happens," Susan said, winding her chiffon scarf around her head and neck. "I've got to go."

13

IT TURNED OUT TO BE MORE DIFFICULT TO WRITE MY father than I had thought. I found, for example, that I didn't want to hurt his feelings. He was my father, after all, even if I'd never met him. Maybe I would be able to meet him some day if I didn't blow my letter. So finally I just said that our next-door neighbor had always been like an uncle (I said father first and crossed that out) and that I would like to stay with him until Mom came home.

I imagine he was a little surprised, but he wrote Fermine and Susan and me all nice letters saying "Sure" and "God Bless," and on the strength of them Fermine became my temporary foster father. It all took about three weeks, and at the end Mom didn't look any closer to coming home. In fact, they had moved her to a private room.

When Fermine got his first foster parent check, he took me shopping, and we blew the whole thing on clothes. Dolly went along to help me create an image, which is easier to do when you can buy half a dozen outfits at once. We decided I was the leather skirt and peasant blouse type. Frontier girl. I had never owned a wardrobe, by which I mean clothes that match and suit me and are all new. The first night I stayed up until four A.M. trying everything on, feeling very much like Annie Oakley; but soon I was just wearing whatever happened to be clean, the same as before the image. It was nice of Fermine, though.

Of course, I had particularly hoped the new look would help with Allan, but he continued to be "distantly affectionate" (Dolly's term), which meant that he spoke when we met at school but never asked me to go bird watching or anywhere else where we might possibly be alone. Dolly said he'd shown himself for the "selfish egotist" he was; but her boyfriend had found himself a girl who could go out on Saturday nights, so Dolly was pretty bitter about all men. I decided Mom and I had embarrassed Allan. Seven closets full of clothes wouldn't have made up for seeing me next to her in that church. After all, who wants to feel sorry for a girlfriend? It wouldn't turn me on, either.

Late one afternoon I was sitting in Fermine's garden watching Fermine press cactus to make a milky juice that he felt contained all essential vitamins. I was remembering the times Allan and I had walked on the beach at that hour, when I looked up and there was Susan in a pink and red flowered chiffon dress. She looked cool and pretty.

"I just came by to see if you'd like to go out to dinner with me," she said.

"How come? Never mind, sure. At a restaurant? What should I wear?"

"Any restaurant you choose. Just put on stockings," she answered lightly. I wondered if Susan was just being friendly. Maybe she got lonely eating by herself night after night. She didn't have a boyfriend so far as I knew. Anyhow, it would help me forget about Allan.

There is only one good restaurant within a 25-mile radius of our town, and it sits way back on a hill overlooking the ocean. That evening the artichoke fields surrounding the restaurant were in purple bloom and even the sunset took on a magenta cast. I had never been there before, in fact I had never been to any restaurant with white linen table cloths, wine goblets, and chandeliers.

I was still taking it all in when, from sheer nervousness, I asked the fatal question.

"When is Mom coming home?"

"How did she look the last time you saw her, April?" Susan shot back.

I didn't answer. She'd been sitting up in the hospital bed pulling out grey hairs and scratching herself, and she hadn't stopped when I came in. I could see why they'd switched her to a private room. Of course, if it hadn't taken them three weeks to get her new glasses, she could have been reading, and things wouldn't have gotten so bad. I didn't mention this to Susan, though, because when I had told Dolly about it, she had said Mom should have hung on to her glasses if she wanted them. For women so basically different, Susan and Dolly said too many of the same things.

Susan reached across the white tablecloth and took my hand. I wanted to pull it away, but was afraid she might think I was mad. Actually, I'd always been sensitive about adults touching me. They took your hand, I'd found, before they broke the bad news. This was particularly true of Susan.

"She needs help, April. She's needed it for a long time. She's been losing touch with reality ever since I've known her. The doctors are sending her to a hospital where she can get fine treatment."

"You've caged her because she isn't like you," I shouted. All the middle-aged customers turned and stared. Our waiter's eyes bored into my soul.

"Don't say that! It's not true. Can't you see? Your mother's been sent to a hospital where they specialize in helping schizophrenics. They know how to help her get well, believe me," Susan whispered. I'd pulled my hand away and hers was still groping over the table.

I kept watching that hand playing with a knife on the table, then a spoon, then the base of a wine goblet. I wasn't listening anymore. I do not even remember what I ate for dinner or whether I ate at all. I do not remember getting home that night.

The next morning I left the house without seeing Fermine. I did not want to see him; but it was strange that no smoke came from his chimney, there was no call for breakfast, and no threat that I would be late to school. He, too, had deserted me. I went back and got ten dollars I'd been saving for a bathing suit. What for I didn't know. But I had a feeling I might need it before the day was over.

My unhappiness deepened quietly until the teacher called on me in fourth period, American history. I had been absorbing the green lawn outside and had no idea what she asked, so I got up and walked out the door and down to the principal's office. I could have continued directly out the front door, but I did not want to be suspended because I didn't know what I would do *without* school. It was my haven, my escape. But not that day.

"My mother's been put in an insane asylum, and I just cannot stay in school today," I told the principal evenly.

I could see that I had shocked her. Her hand reached

out for the telephone. Would she call Susan? The doctor? I don't think the school even knew I was staying with Fermine.

"Maybe, if I could go lie down in the nurse's office for a little while," I said quickly.

"Yes, of course, that's an excellent idea, April. Then you'll feel better. I'm sure your mother—will be—completely well—very soon," she said, taking her hand off the phone.

What did she know about it? Had she performed an examination—or an autopsy—or even asked me what was wrong with her? Maybe she thought my mother must be all right because I was on the honor roll.

I nodded, evaded her comforting hands, and started dutifully toward the nurse's office, turned left at the crucial fork in the hall, and walked quickly down the steps instead, past the green lawn, and ran.

Only after I'd caught the Greyhound bus for San Luis did I feel safe. The principal couldn't catch me there.

I leaned back and let our town pass in a series of kaleidoscopic technicolors, focusing only when we finally hit the countryside. Beyond the packing sheds and farm worker's shacks, we wound into the open country, green hills on one side and cliffs dropping off to the Pacific Ocean on the other. Patches of lupine and poppies dotted the fields, apparently left

118

alone by the herds of cattle watching our bus.

In San Luis I took the first local bus on the corner by the Greyhound station. There is no way for me to guess how long I rode that bus except for a vague sensation of seeing the city several times. I was enjoying myself. Just so long as the bus kept moving, I was free from thinking of anything. I began to fidgit if we stopped anywhere for long.

Once a middle-aged lady with a grey permanent and too much powder asked me where I was going. I thought I might have to move, which would spoil everything. I opened my mouth and found I couldn't talk, so I turned my face to the window and eventually she huffed and moved. Still, it was frightening to think I might not be able to speak if I wanted to, even if she had moved.

Gradually I realized that the bus driver was watching me, had been watching me for the last couple of trips. Of course, he and I were the only people on the bus a good half of each run. But this forced me to realize that I would have to get off the bus eventually, even though I carefully went up and paid an extra fare every time I heard him turn the cranks that tallied the fare and changed our destination. I was paying my way. I wondered if my mother would have taken busses instead of walking if there'd been busses in our town. I wondered if she'd taken a bus out to the little chapel where Allan and I found her. Did she see what

I was seeing? Was I staring as she did?

I pushed the thoughts back into the oblivion of rolling wheels and open spaces; I was safe from the world and rolling endlessly on.

Then the bus stopped, and the driver was talking to me. I forced myself to listen, though I knew I could not answer him. Maybe he'd think I was a deaf-mute.

"I said, this is going to be the last run, kid. Where do you want me to let you off?"

"But I paid my way." I heard my voice with surprise. So I only lost my voice with smelly grey-haired ladies? I could talk to bus drivers at least.

"Did anybody say you didn't? Look, kid, I don't know what your problem is but I've been on this damn bus since noon and, if you don't mind, I'd like to get home for supper." He sat down next to me and put his arm lightly across the back of the seat. I noticed it was getting dark outside. I recognized the filling station next to us as one on the outskirts of town, but was it at the end of the line?

"Want to talk about it?"

No, I didn't, but he smelled good, of a spicy shaving lotion, and I found his nearness comforting, so I nodded.

"Well, shoot. What's eating you, beautiful?" He moved his arm down around my shoulder and I leaned my head against him. I could have fallen asleep.

"Let's have it, honey," he said, rubbing my hair softly with his hand. I remember that his hand had calluses, though I have no memory of the man at all, not even any idea of his age, for I answered his question.

"My mother's schizophrenic, and yesterday they put her in an asylum." I thought the word "cage" but did not want to shock him. Susan's word—hospital—was a copout.

He jumped up so quickly that I fell over on the seat. I remember the calloused hands stretched wide and stiff and repelled, as if I had leprosy.

"Good God!" he said. "Don't I have the run, though? Don't that take the cake?"

I lay sprawled on the seat, and he looked menacing, towering over me. But the seat was still warm where he'd sat, and I lay with my cheek against the warmth. The memory of his arm around me clung side by side with his natural shrinking from us. I hated to sit up and lose the last vestige of that warmth. It was beginning to get dark. I started to cry, ashamed to have him see me cry, but unable to stop, unable to sit up, unable to pretend any more. I had nowhere in the whole world to go.

"Oh, come on now, kid. Most of us have crazy mothers. They just ain't caught up with 'em yet, is all. Now be a doll and just tell me where you live, and I'll take you home. I'll take you right to your own door. Just tell me where it is. Please."

I gave him Susan's address mechanically, still lying on that warm seat, wet now with my tears. I couldn't think of any other address.

"Well, thank the Lord for small favors," he said and started toward the front of the bus. The bus squeaked with his footsteps. I sat up when he turned on the engine.

Suddenly the lights went on. That made all the difference. Only the bus was lighted, and the world outside was all dark. It must be like that at night where she was: small like the inside of a bus, and closed in.

"Well, here we are, kid. Is this on the level where you live? Want me to come in with you?"

I saw that there were lights on in Susan's apartment.

The bus doors folded open, but they didn't fool me. This bus was my cage and I couldn't get out. Still, I looked hopefully at the driver. If he came, maybe I could get out. I nodded. The driver and I left the bus together.

"Now, please go home. I'm all right now."

"Sure?" he asked but he was already turning back to his bus. He'd had a long day.

I rang Susan's bell.

14

SUSAN'S BUZZER OPENED THE DOOR, AND I STARTED UP
the dark stairs. My knees kept buckling and I wondered if I would make it to the top stair and the
lighted room beyond. I wanted sleep so badly I would
have curled up there on the stairs, if they had been a
little wider. If only Susan wouldn't insist on under-
standing, would let me lie down on that wonderful
blue velvet couch and sleep for ten hours first. I heard
voices. She had company! I huddled in the dark, cling-
ing to the banister. I had to get out. I had to leave the
promise of those warm lights and go back to walk in
the night.

"Who is it?" Susan loomed from the room above,
leaning over the railing, her fair hair and slender fig-

ure silhouetted, a boundary between light and dark. I flattened myself against the wall. "I can't see who it is. I'm afraid the hall light's out. Could you——"

"Susan, I've never seen you without glasses. What have you done with them?" I asked, and I was ashamed of the way my voice shook. Did she throw them away because the world looked so much softer without them? Like Mom? Oh, I hoped not. Not Susan, too.

A man was coming down the stairs! I wanted to run, but I stood frozen, one arm over my face.

"April, where the hell have you been? We've combed the county for you. Then we thought maybe you were with Fermine."

"Allan?"

I didn't even ask what he was doing there when he'd never even met Susan. I just fell on him, nearly tumbling us both down those stairs. His hand braced against the wall, the muscles taut with the effort of holding me.

"I'm so tired. Please let me sleep first," I said.

"As long as you want," Allan replied.

"Oh, I'm so glad you came here, so glad you're all right," Susan called, still leaning precariously.

"Are you hurt? Never mind, I'll carry you." I think Allan kissed my hair as he hauled me up to Susan's blue couch. Maybe I only imagined he kissed me or maybe it was a momentary lapse. As he said the next afternoon when he was stringing our kites:

"The thing is, I really like you, but I don't want to

get too involved, not with anyone. That day with your mother was too heavy, too—sad, that's not the right word, but all I can think of. I'm sorry—no, April, let me finish—I have to say this at the start so we both understand. There's high school and college and veterinary school and, most of the time, all I really want is to sit out here flying kites with a girl like you, with you, really. But I can't take care of animals, the way I want, at least, without going on to school for years and years. And I know positively that I do not want to stay home and farm. The truth is, I *like* to see a bird able to fly with a wing I've set. I don't know. Do I make any sense at all? Maybe I just have a big ego—birdman of the world—I don't know."

Allan looked out toward the ocean, his mouth still working silently. The kites and string and jackknife lay in a patch of wild flowers beside him. We were sitting on a broad mesa bluff, a sunny meadow of lupine and buttercup overlooking the farms, our town, and the fan of live sand dunes that separated it all from the ocean. Allan had chosen the bluff because there were neither trees nor telephone wires to trap our kites. What little breeze there was at that time of day came from the south and would help lift the kites.

Allan turned back, facing me, still unhappy, forcing me to think about us, and how could I? He had this blueprint of what he wanted to do all his life, and I thought it was great. I didn't want to get in the way but—we didn't have to be hermits until we were old enough to get married, did we?

"Couldn't we go back—to how it was—before? I don't want to get involved either. I don't have something I have to do like being a veterinarian, but I do have a dream. I don't even know if I can do it, but—well—the reason I want to work in the beans this summer is for ballet lessons. Don't tell Dolly. She teases me already—and it takes ten years and it will all probably come to nothing." What I was saying wasn't the way I wanted it to be, but I was so tired I wasn't even sure what Allan meant by involved. I might have asked, but I was afraid Allan might just take off and never return. He didn't sound too sure of what he meant either. He didn't want to be hemmed in, I decided.

Allan smiled, relieved. "We could try," he said. "Which kite do you want? And—April—I'm glad about the dancing."

They looked alike to me. Both were red, white, and blue plasticized paper shields backed with wooden crosses. I shrugged and went back to tearing strips off an old sheet and knotting them for tails.

"The one that flies best," I said.

"Greedy."

The first kite Allan sent up faltered badly at first, careening crazily from side to side, pulling the string out but never gaining height.

"That's a drunken kite," I said, laughing, as Allan reeled it back in.

"Your fault. Needs more tail. Old neckties make the best tails, but my dad never wears them."

We added another 3 feet and tried again. That time he had more trouble getting started and had to run back and forth across the little meadow, cutting a crumpled path through the wild flowers. But, once up, the kite flew straight skyward and out toward the sea, taking all the string on the ball and straining at the knot Allan made around the scrap of wood he used for a handle.

"It's like a butterfly; I feel as if it's me up there, floating," I whispered.

"No butterfly I ever saw could fly that high," Allan replied proudly. He gave me the handle and started to run with the other kite.

We had a good hour with both kites soaring, sitting close together while they drifted like gliders through the blue and round-clouded sky. We held the ends of our strings, saying little, warmed by the sun, emptying out. I sat within the circle of Allan's free arm and leaned against him, feeling much as I had when the bus driver put his arm around me, except that Allan knew all about me and still held tight. The day before seemed a distant memory, one that left me limp but was already hazy.

Promptly at four o'clock, as the mail train ribboned across our valley, hooting its whistle at our station, the wind shifted. It veered in from the sea, jerking our kites violently. It was the same every day.

"You can clock that wind by the mail train, every time," Allan said proudly, reeling in his kite. It was the kind of remark Fermine would make.

"Time to pull the clothes off the line or they'll be sandy." I laughed, wrapping string around my wooden handle and hanging on tight. It was easy to lose a kite in such a gusty wind, and I wanted to come and fly kites with Allan again. My kite kept drifting toward Allan's, and I kept tugging it back. Finally they did tangle.

"Time to go." Allan grinned.

I almost said something about only the kites being involved, but Allan wasn't the kind of person you teased about important things, so I was quiet. Also, there was something I had to ask him when the kites were secured.

We were nearly home before I could bring myself to talk about it.

"How did you find out—yesterday?"

"Miss Morgan called Dolly after the school called her," he said reluctantly. "No one could find Fermine."

"He drove down to see her and didn't get back until time for breakfast this morning," I said. I couldn't even say Mom. Even so, the pure delight of the afternoon was gone. I kept trying to think of something to say that would bring back the kites, dissolve the heavy silence.

Allan snapped on the radio. When western music

came on, we listened for a few miles before he reached out and turned it off and then, pulling the car off the road, stopped.

He turned and faced me. We looked at each other a long moment, and then he leaned over and kissed me.

15

I LOOKED OUT THE WINDOW TO SEE THE MORNING AND found Fermine washing his car, a sure sign of a trip. I knew I couldn't put it off any longer anyway. I'd run out of alibis. The day before had been the last day of school. We didn't start picking beans for two weeks. I would have to go. However, I was going to do it my way.

When Fermine rang the cow bell for breakfast, I was ready. I collected a sweater, my purse, and locked the door as I left our house. I probably wouldn't need the sweater. It was going to be a scorcher, especially through the valley stretch.

"Today we are going to see your mother," Fermine said the minute I walked into his kitchen.

"Good morning to you, too," I answered.

"You must go if you want her to get well. She is desperate."

"I *am* going. Today. But I am going by myself," I said firmly, taking a roundtrip Greyhound bus ticket for the town nearest the hospital out of my purse and handing it to him. It was crumpled because it had been in my purse a long time, over a mouth. I had bought it with the last of the money I'd saved for the swimsuit.

He patted his pockets until he found the one with his reading glasses and, putting them on, read over the ticket carefully. Then he handed it back and, going to the stove, dished out two helpings of Spanish rice, my favorite breakfast.

"The sapling that will not bend must break," he said finally.

"But by definition a sapling does bend unless someone breaks it. I want to talk to her alone."

"It is three miles from the bus station to the hospital."

"I walk almost that far every day to school and back."

"I promised her I would come."

"I'll tell her you are coming tomorrow."

"A waste of good money," he said and, slamming the door, went outside.

I held my breath. So far Fermine and I had avoided any obedience rules. This was our first confrontation since he'd had any title over me, and I didn't know what I'd do if he insisted I go with him. I did know. I *had* to see her by myself, whatever happened. I could see him striding up and down the cement walk that led in a straight line from the door to the back gate. Then he stopped by the peach tree and started picking off blighted leaves. The curl was a choice enemy. He could be at that all morning. If he made me miss my bus—— It wouldn't work, that's all. He couldn't make me go with him! He could make me miss my bus, though, because he would send me away if I left without permission, and he knew I'd never risk that. It wasn't only that I had nowhere else to live but also that Fermine was like family, the only family I had left.

Quite suddenly he stopped, wiped his hands on his blue overalls, and came back.

"You must be home by dark and no excuses," he said fiercely.

"I'll come in on the 6:40." I'd won. I'd won!

"I will meet the bus. Now, get in the car or you will miss this one. Drink your cocoa first. Use your napkin. Do you have money?"

I was delighted with myself all the way to the hospital, but once I reached the waiting room, I began to wish Fermine were with me. Maybe I was just tired from being jolted around on a smokey bus for three hours. It wasn't that the hospital waiting room was so terribly different from the Greyhound bus station. In both places everyone was covered with bundles, ate

132

constantly, and smelled of cheap perfume, old pop-corn, and garlic. It was just that in the hospital I kept worrying about who was crazy and who was not. I could have used Fermine's shrewd eye because I didn't do too well. Every time I spotted a particularly wild-eyed man, he turned out to be a husband trying to figure out what to say next. Finally I realized that the ones who rolled their tongues, stared like my mother, and shuffled when they walked, were patients.

Then I had nothing else to do. I'd been waiting half an hour. I wanted to ask the starched nurse guarding the locked door what was taking so long, but I caught her giving me the once over, so it didn't seem like a safe idea. Maybe she was wondering if I were a pa-tient?

The door squeaked like a rusty guillotine. You would think they would oil the hinges at least. An-other old lady came through, somebody's mother. Two hundred heads looked up, stopped eating, bobbed down. I had spent what money Fermine had given me on cigarettes and instant coffee and chocolate-covered cherries for Mom instead of on lunch, and the smell of chicken was almost more than I could bear. Where *was* she?

Then she came. She stooped, and her hand shook as she brushed back her hair and peered out like Geron-imo, looking for her April, her baby. She didn't look like anyone I'd ever seen before or ever intended to see again and there she was bearing down on me. I prayed not to throw up.

Had it really been only two months since I'd seen her? It seemed like a lifetime. But she *was* wearing her glasses.

"Ah, darling. So beautiful. Ah, God," she said, folding me in her arms.

"Come home, Mom, I want you home," I moaned. How had *that* gotten out? Hadn't everyone warned me not to upset her? Apparently she hadn't heard me. That was a break. I looked up, and she was staring wildly about, hunting for something or someone.

"Ah, Mrs. Moore, there you are. Here is my big girl, April. Would you believe she was an incubator baby? Mrs. Moore has a son who was in an incubator, too, April. Isn't that a coincidence?" Mom said, peering at the nurse on duty by the locked door, the one who'd already looked me over.

"Mom, please! Don't!"

"She's a fine strapping girl now, a fine young girl," the nurse said, looking as if she thought I were anything but. "Well, I'm off duty now, and I'd best be getting home to my own boy," she added, walking briskly off before Mom had a chance to get into any more detail about my birth.

"Let's go out on the lawn. It's a nice day. Wait until you see how I've got the house fixed up," I said, dragging her out of the room, past anyone else who might have had an incubator baby. If I just kept putting one foot in front of the other over and over again, sooner or later I would get out of the waiting room, away from the locked door and through the other one, the one that led to the freedom of the garden. If I didn't look up, my mother couldn't introduce me to any more of her big happy family. All I had to do was keep moving.

"Mrs. Moore is a good nurse, April. She's—gentle. You know some of them are pretty rough."

My stomach sank, but I didn't answer. We had to get out of there. I had a pass in my hand that said we could walk on the grounds, and that was what we were going to do. Finally we were in the long arched hallway that led past the administration offices, the reception desk, Coke machines, another waiting room, and down broad stairs to sunlight. The building looked like an old monastery, and I pretended we were two musketeers fleeing through endless catacombs to freedom. I could hear Mom talking behind me, but I did not stop to listen.

I stumbled down the stairs and flopped on the lawn. Only then did I look up to see if Mom were still with me.

"Ah, April, still the efficient little organizer," Mom said, smiling gently as she sank down beside me, adjusting her dress self consciously. If only she weren't so nervous. She had never seemed so nervous before.

I shoved the carton of cigarettes and the coffee and the box of chocolate-covered cherries toward her. I had forgotten how soft her face was. Most older women had hard lines in their faces, as if they had been mad at the world for years, but she didn't. She fingered the satin ribbons on the candy box absently, looking at me.

"Is it lonely in the house all by yourself? Fermine says you are a real little housewife."

"He says he'll come tomorrow."

"Poor Fermine."

"That's what he says about you."

She laughed then. It started low and joyous and ended in a bitter cackle.

I shivered.

"I still have this sore throat," she said, turning the presents over, not opening them.

"Cigarettes," I suggested.

"Yes, a cigarette would be good."

I handed her the matches. Then I lay back on the lawn, relaxing in its cool sponginess. I watched her light the cigarette and take a long satisfying drag. She bent forward, toward me, and her hair fell over her face. Suddenly she reached up and yanked a grey hair. Just one. She held the single strand of hair between her thumb and a cigarette stained forefinger for a moment, considering it, and then dropped it to the lawn. When she turned away, I reached over, took the hair, and put it in my purse.

"How are you?" I asked quickly.

She was watching a toddler in a family nearby. The baby would take a few steps, fall, look around and pick himself up, and start again. She sighed and turned back to me.

"Why am I here? Do you know, April?"

I shook my head slowly. Bad luck. Because they caught you, I thought. Because we aren't like Dolly's grandmother, dusting all day. There was the night-walking and the staring, of course. I wasn't supposed to upset her so what could I say to a question like that? What had the doctors said to her? I shrugged. I couldn't stand to think about it anymore.

All the while my mother watched me intently. "This is a terrible place," she whispered. "I never knew a place would matter so much, but it's so closed in here. I don't even see the sunrise."

I thought of her bed at home, turned to celebrate the morning.

We both stared out at the mountains. Beyond the lawns and the formal Spanish gardens and the low adobe buildings with red tile roofs—the Spanish style made the bars at the windows seem part of the archi-tecture—were truck gardens and walnut groves and finally the Sierra Nevada Mountains, snowcapped even in June. They looked cold and remote.

"Hey, Mary, how about a smoke or two? You got treats, I see, but me, I ain't a mother." I jerked around to see a tall spare old man in denim overalls standing behind us. How long had he been there?

"John, help yourself and welcome. I'd like you to meet my daughter, April. John has been a good friend to me here. Would you believe this big girl is mine, John?"

"Well, she'll soon be big enough to come and take you out of this hellhole, right kid?" His voice sounded ugly, as if he were really saying it was my fault she was there. He was toothless, and tobacco juice stained his beard and the ancient grey suit vest he wore over his overalls. I turned my back on him, hoping he'd go away. I could hear my mother ripping open the carton of cigarettes. How many packs was she giving him? My lunch. I could taste the hamburger I would have gotten.

"Well, Mary, see you around. Kid can't talk, huh?"

"Get out of here, you, and leave her a couple of lousy things for herself. I went without lunch to buy them," I said, close to crying.

"Ain't that *too* bad?" he said, dripping sarcasm.

"John, please. We've only got this afternoon."

The old man turned and stalked off without another word. When he was a few feet away he turned and, catching me watching him, spat.

"His son brought him here eight years ago," she said quietly.

"I can see why."

"Ah, please don't get hard, April."

"Well, I'm not his son."

We only had another half hour. I wanted to ask what the doctors said when they'd told her she was coming there, if she wanted some clothes, a hundred

138

questions. And I wanted her to ask me about Allan and my plans for the summer. I wanted to forget what she'd said, the question she'd asked. Maybe it would have been better to come with Fermine.

"I have to catch a bus soon," I said.

16

I COULD NOT REMEMBER WHY I HAD WANTED TO SEE my mother alone. We sat across from each other on the lawn while she watched a baby learn to walk and I tried to make conversation. She answered me absently, as if we might have been strangers in a dentist's office. Soon I would have to walk three miles back to town and take the Greyhound bus home. I could have saved the bus fare toward a new sweater if I'd come with Fermine.

"Do you want me to bring you some clothes?" I heard in my own voice the exasperation that had once made me so mad when I heard it in Susan's voice as she talked to my mother. "Mo-ther, please. Can't you watch the baby after I go?"

"The baby will go, too," she said with a sigh and turned back to me. "There are no babies here." She took off her new glasses and laid them on the lawn. Maybe I looked softer to her without them.

"Well, there aren't any babies at home either, and you didn't seem to miss them. Besides, someone must have a baby here, out of five thousand people."

"A girl on the ward has been here ten years and she's never heard of a case. She says there was a woman who carried a Raggedy Ann doll around and claimed it was her natural baby, but that was all." She started to light a cigarette but her hands shook so that the match went out. I lit another and held her hand steady.

"Ah, April, thank you. Always the practical one. You can't imagine how I miss you and Fermine. And how is Thor?"

"Thor? You can't possibly miss Thor!" I started to laugh. That sadistic Doberman had to be the least lovable dog in the whole world. I would have been delighted to see and hear the last of that biting bully. "As a matter of fact, I haven't seen Thor lately. He hasn't even been howling at the moon—but I can't say I miss him."

"I do. He was so vulnerable, with a different voice for each complaint. They made him mean by keeping him locked up all the time. Poor Thor," she added in a whisper.

"Poor Thor has always been ready to make a meal·

of your only daughter's leg, you know. However, I'll tell him you miss him. It's time to go, Mom," I added gently.

I knew she'd be unhappy, but I wasn't prepared for the fear in her widened eyes. "No, not yet! April. Listen to me. Today is the longest day in the year—June 21, did you remember—and tomorrow every day gets shorter, and the nights are the worst here. I don't think I can go through the long winter nights listening to them all suffer." She looked up at the sky as if she expected instant darkness. "One woman goes shuffling between the beds on her poor little feet all night, back and forth, back and forth."

"I'll come back."

"Oh, God, no, not yet!"

"Fermine will be here tomorrow," I said desperately, reaching out a hand and pulling her up. I gathered the cigarettes and coffee and chocolate-covered cherries and stuffed them back in the brown shopping bag. Then I remembered her glasses, cast away on the lawn.

"Here, Mom. Don't forget your glasses. You need them to read. I'll bring some mysteries."

She was crying. I kept hold of her hand, but I did not look at her again until we were through the maze of halls and back in the waiting room. Her face was streaked with drying tears, but she was quiet. She stared out into the flowered curtains and seemed to have forgotten I was there.

I saw nurses threading their way through the crowd, tapping patients on the arm and rounding them up before the locked door. Have you ever seen quarter horses cut certain cattle from a herd and nudge them off to the sidelines? They do it at rodeos all the time. It was like that.

I kept thinking there must be something terribly important that I'd forgotten to say. Or ask? I couldn't remember. She hadn't seemed interested in anything, except——

I felt a gentle pressure, like the tap in a game of tag, on my own arm. I looked up into the eyes of a nurse in a starched cap and a set smile. I wasn't surprised. It was only the gentle brown eyes that threw me. She had eyes like Allan Sebastian. I would never see Allan again.

Why did my mother go on standing there? Did someone have to stick her with a pin? She was free. The nurse had tapped *my* arm! Visiting hours are over; get out of here while the getting's good, I thought.

"Ah, well, take care of yourself, darling. I'm ready now, Mrs. Brady," I heard my mother say. The nurse shifted her hand from my arm to my mother's without any change of expression. The plastic smile and the warm eyes remained exactly the same. It was just that the red fingernails were biting into my mother's blue sweater instead of my bare arm. That was all? Maybe the nurse was a robot programmed to collect fifteen bodies and deliver them to the dining room so the routine could continue.

"Come next week. You're all I have. I'd like a few cans of evaporated milk if you can manage it," Mom called from the door, stretching out her arms and blowing me kisses.

I stood trembling, palsied, until my mother was herded through the door. I saw the nurse turn the patients over to someone else and come back into the room. I think I screamed then. I ran back through the long halls and out across the lawns, down to the crossroad flanked in poplar trees, before I stopped to see if anyone was following me. No one. I turned my back on the hospital buildings and ignored the swoosh of passing cars. Visiting hours were over.

Below the road, fields of ripe string beans stretched in long neat rows ending in stacks of boxes. I felt in my hands what it must be like to snap each bean from its vine, drop it in a gunny sack, root among the lush growth for the next, and finally dump the sack into one of those waiting boxes. I knew the process, though I had never picked, and at that moment it seemed a wonderful miracle that I was freely walking along the road and would soon be picking beans like those with Dolly and Allan.

But I had to walk faster. It was a long way yet, that town where I could catch the Greyhound bus. A heat haze hung over its cluster of houses, giving it the shimmer of a mirage in the distance. But I had been there and smelled the stale popcorn and old perfume in the station, and all I had to do was run a little and I would be in that crowded warmth again.

Fermine would be furious if I missed the bus. Maybe there wasn't another one before morning. I had no idea what time it was. The wind sweeping down the valley and rustling the tall poplars was turning cold. Maybe I had already missed the bus.

But that could not be. I had to catch *that* bus! Fermine was waiting, and he would have a hot dinner for me. I had to catch that bus and never come back again.

17

Two weeks later we started picking the Sebastian beans. Sunrise poured down from the mesa behind us and reflected back from the sand dunes rising at the other end of the valley, not yet touching the long rows of string beans, darkly fragrant and so thick that I could see only a thin ribbon of brown earth between rows. It was a big field, big enough so that in the week it would take to pick the ripe beans the blossoms we'd left would become beans, almost ready to pick. With luck and normal sunshine I'd have work all summer, rotating between the bean field and a similar one planted to peas, picking them again and again until the vines withered, exhausted in what Fermine called their instinct to reproduce. And work was definitely what I wanted, the best way to be exhausted and rich. I'd been marking days off on the calendar, telling myself that once I was working my mother couldn't expect me to do anything else; neither to free her nor to visit her. And there I was! I breathed deeply and dug my toes into the cold sandy earth.

We stood huddled together at one corner of the field behind a 5-foot stack of gunnysacks. A cold wind ripped over us. Fermine, in his shirt sleeves, crouched, lining wooden crates with oiled paper. He was there, as a favor, to help with the first picking because of a rush order from a supermarket chain; but he was anxious to finish the job and get back to his own asparagus. Dolly sat next to him, crosslegged, head erect, eyes closed, hands folded. She was practicing yoga, and I was glad to see she was human enough to have goosepimples.

Mr. Sebastian, an enormous barrel of a man who laughed a lot, looked over his fields as he finished a cigar. Allan stood next to his father and kept blowing on his cupped hands and putting them over his ears. He'd had a mastoid years before, and I wondered if maybe his ears were sensitive to the cold. He smiled as he caught me watching and moved over closer.

"Will your father hate me if I don't make it to the end of the first row?" I knew better than to ask if his ear hurt. Allan did not like "smother-mothers."

"Just take it slow and steady, the way I showed you," Allan replied, pressing my hand briefly.

"Are these the same beans you kept trying to save last winter?"

"Replanted for the fourth time. How did you know?"

"She spent whole weekends watching from my window, that's how," Dolly said, her eyes still closed, her hands still folded over crossed legs.

Dolly's voice was like those bell-chime doorbells. It hung on after she'd spoken, and set up vibrations somehow, so that no one else said anything. Personally, I was too mad. She knew how Allan would feel about being spied on. I could see Fermine and Mr. Sebastian exchange a grin.

"Paid off even if we did lose that batch. We'll still be the first field harvested in south county, thanks to Allan," Mr. Sebastian said finally, picking up several gunnysacks and handing one to each of us.

"Except that it was peas we planted that first time and beans we're harvesting," Allan added, grinning at his father.

"Man's got a right to change his mind—and both make the old cash register jingle. Many's a time I was ready to head for the fireplace and my slippers, and you said to come on, you'd help me trench. Well, early bird gets the worm. Come on, Mahatma Gandhi, off your butt. Yes, I mean you, Doll." Mr. Sebastian reached out a hand and pulled Dolly to her feet, giving her a hug, a gunnysack, and a shove toward the beans.

148

"Yoga would make a new man of you," Dolly called over her shoulder, as she crouched and expertly started snapping beans.

"What's wrong with the man I've worked fifty years to become, Angel?" Mr. Sebastian asked as he took the row next to Dolly. "Get to work, son."

We'd agreed that Allan and I wouldn't work together until after the first picking, so Fermine could help me learn. I was being paid at the same rate as Dolly and Allan, and I hadn't their experience, so I needed all the help Fermine could give.

Fermine paced his picking to mine, reaching over and working my side of the vine from time to time so I could keep up. He had long lean fingers, and they knew which beans were big enough, which dense vines hid filled pods. I could hear him chewing charcoal, which he felt whitened all teeth, even "store-bought" teeth.

I could also hear Dolly laughing with Allan and his father. Mr. Sebastian made no secret of his preference for Dolly, but there was nothing I could do about it. I couldn't keep up with them yet.

I wouldn't have to worry if only Dolly would choose another boyfriend. She could go out once a week since she had turned fifteen, and she went, all right, but never twice with the same guy. Allan told her she missed Chris Roberts, and she looked him straight in the eye and said she needed someone who could tickle her brain more than that dumb athlete.

Allan being the brightest guy around, I knew I had to learn to pick beans, but fast.

I had always thought of myself as tall and gangly, but the bean vines grew over my head. Fermine, who is six foot two, stood on the other side of my row, and all I could see of him was the top of his straw hat and the gnarled hand that reached over, groped through the green and silver leaves, and picked the top part of my row. I was lost in a world of beans. The row stretched forever. Rabbit tracks and the webbed imprint of a bird's claws ran between the rows, but I saw neither of them.

Gradually I developed a kind of rhythm, so that, picking from the bottom, I could almost keep up with Fermine's reappearing hand. I took off my cap and then my sweater. My fingers ached, tips rubbed raw. I wished I'd brought a watch. Fermine, I knew, would hate my asking the time. The only time that mattered to him was the time it would take to finish the entire field. He sang softly, old Spanish songs I half-knew, and I wondered if he'd ever thought of being a singer. He was the one man I knew who was always either humming or singing.

The only break came when Fermine took our full gunnysacks back to the end of the row and dumped them in the packing boxes. Then I could lie on the ground, resting my aching arms, and look at the sky. I would listen to Mr. Sebastian and Dolly and Allan laughing and talking, and knew I must be the only one who ached, who choked on the dust.

"You pick well. We will finish this row in half an hour," Fermine said once, bringing me another empty gunnysack.

"And then?"

"The next row."

"I'll die. My arms will drop off. What time is it, Fermine?"

"Nine-thirty," he said, grinning.

"Oh, no! It *must* be later than that. When do we eat lunch?" There was a fresh burst of laughter from Dolly, and Fermine must have seen me look over.

"Do not worry," he said. "There is happiness in the eyes when Allan looks to *you*."

"I'm his little sister," I said, but I was thinking of the happiness in the eyes. Was it true? Had Fermine really seen something in the way Allan looked at me? "He doesn't want to get involved."

Fermine smiled and nodded. "We all try to run away, don't we?" he asked, handing me the gunny-sack and starting down the row.

"Just who are you really talking about and what do you mean by that? Wait a minute, Fermine. You can't just say something like that and run away."

Fermine turned and stared at me. There was no laughter and no gentleness in his face. He spit out the charcoal.

"You know."

"That isn't the same thing at all, and you know it.

I *can't* ever go back to see Mom, not until she comes home, and you may as well know it. I really can't; not won't—can't."

Fermine stared at me. I waited, but he said nothing.

"Every day you make some hint, and I'm sick and tired of it. Every day it's when are we going, or do you want to start early Saturday so you can be home by afternoon, or your mother is very lonely, or, always something. These last two weeks have been sheer nightmare, and I can't take it any longer, so we may as well have it out. Do you want to know what happened when I went down to see her? Do you really have to know?"

He nodded, shifting his weight from one foot to the other, but never taking his eyes off me.

"Well, I can't go because they'll keep me there, that's why. You don't believe it, do you? Well, it's true. You know when they go around sorting out the patients to make them go back to the wards after visiting hours?" I stopped to catch my breath.

"Yes, I remember."

"The nurse did *not* tap Mom on the shoulder, she tapped *me*. It was *me* she was going to take back to that ward and lock up. And—I don't want—to go."

Fermine's arms were around me, and I was crying. "So you can see it's just impossible." I sobbed.

"Poor Mary in such a place. Stupid nurse doesn't even know the people. How can they help her when they don't even see——"

Fermine kept muttering against my hair, and I could only catch some of what he said. It was some time before I calmed down enough to realize that none of it had to do with me. He was only worried about my mother.

"How about *me?* Can you see why I can't go back."

"In a stupid place like that she needs to see you."

"She touched me. That nurse will take me, keep me, she *will!*" I whispered.

"You think those hospitals have so much money, they take people in off the streets? It costs lots of money for doctors and nurses. Why does that Susan want you to live in my spare room—because it costs them less, that's why. It's cheaper for the state that you are a foster child. Don't worry. They never take you. Too much trouble, money. Also, I would burn that place down. That stupid nurse was just too stuck up to wear her glasses and see you at all," Fermine finished, drawing a stick figure of the nurse, with glasses, in the sand next to us.

"But I must have had the look. She must know I should be there, don't you think?"

"How? She never even met you. She just doesn't know her people. But you're such a chicken, how come you didn't just go with her. You knew Mr. Sebastian needed you to pick beans?" Fermine grinned, but I couldn't smile or answer right away. I looked down at my hands, remembering my mother blowing kisses as I left.

"What happened?" he asked again.

"Mom said—she was ready to go. That nurse, she just shifted her smiling hand to Mom's shoulder as if only the numbers counted."

Fermine nodded. He stepped back and held me at arm's length. He scratched in his beard as we stared at each other. And finally he sighed. "Look, April. That dumb nurse was thinking would she cook pork chops or maybe a piece of steak for her dinner when she got off duty. Maybe her feet hurt. All you had to do is say no. That is all it took. You sure know how to say no to me. Your mother is a wonderful woman, but she has trouble saying yes or no. You and I, though, we're mean old goats, and we know we got to say no every day we live in this crazy world. Right? Enough! Now we get back to work?"

He squeezed my shoulder for a moment. Then he smiled and turned and walked quickly down the row. I could hear him snapping the beans and dropping them in the sack, as steadily as though nothing had interrupted him. I stood between the rows, waiting to see his hand appear over the top of the vines, and when it did, I squatted by my side of his row and slowly, mechanically, I started to work.

"He just doesn't understand," I said aloud, but I felt oddly comforted. He would burn the place down, if necessary, to rescue me. I'd never thought of *anyone* helping me but, of course, Fermine would!

18

AFTER A COUPLE OF WEEKS I BEGAN TO FEEL THAT I
had been picking beans all my life, that my days had
always started at sunrise in the cool fields and ended
when the four o'clock mail train shot through our
quiet valley, its eerie whistle our quitting signal. There
is a rhythm to picking, and once I found it, my
muscles healed and I could pace Dolly and Allan, and
talk besides. The three of us were alone most of the
time; Mr. Sebastian returned to running the farm
once the first picking was over, and Fermine went
back to harvesting his own fields. I seldom thought of
the beans until the end of the morning when I'd
stretch out my calloused fingers, look over the bursting
gunnysacks, and know the beans that filled them were

ripe and without dirt or leaves and would, therefore, bring a good price. Every other week we moved to the pea fields and picked the low bush peas, squatting like kangaroos. Even Mr. Sebastian said I was becoming an "experienced hand," a "natural-born dirt farmer" and "tolerable for a girl."

It was our habit to swim in the creek before lunch and then play blackjack on a broad flat rock until Mr. Sebastian called us back to the fields. Willows lined the creek on either side, giving us a sort of room, one we shared with a covey of quail who would glance uneasily at us, hurry Charlie Chaplin like across the path, pecking frantically in the dust, and finally disappear single file into the willow thicket.

Then one day, as I was drowsily watching the quail while Dolly and Allan played out a hand of double solitaire, I heard Dolly shout at Allan.

"All right, all right, I reckon you don't even admit to second sight, do you?"

"You mean, like a seance?" Allan asked.

The very idea sent a cold shiver down my spine. And there was no sarcasm in Allan's question. He was interested. I saw him lean forward eagerly. Dolly must have caught that, too, because her eyes were wide and spooked as she answered.

"Like having this absolute feeling of talking with someone you've never known or being in a strange town and turning the corner and knowing you'll find a movie playing this certain picture that you never even knew existed. You know?"

Allan nodded. "My dad, one day he got this weird feeling, and so he left the fields just like that in the middle of the morning and rushed into the kitchen, and my mother was passed out cold on the floor. She'd had a heart attack, and the doctor said she wouldn't have made it if they hadn't gotten her to the hospital right then."

"It makes you wonder, doesn't it?" Dolly whispered.

"Have you ever been to the fortune teller? You know, the old woman who reads palms and cards in town? I always wondered what it would be like."

"Allan, I'm surprised at you!" Dolly giggled nervously. "Plumb surprised. Let's go. Maybe she can tell me what to do about my sagging love life."

"That's easy. Try Chris again."

"Anyone who would date that giggling mongoloid Mr. Christopher Roberts has been seen with lately couldn't possibly be for me. Besides, I learn a lot playing the field." Dolly raised one eyebrow.

"Suit yourself. You're the one griping about sagging love. Chris just happened to ask about doubling sometime." Allan shrugged.

"Not me, he hasn't. If—let's ask the fortune teller. April will come, too, won't you, sleeping beauty? Come on, we can go tomorrow. It's Saturday. Freedom day."

"I'm not so sure I want to know the future. You

can count me out," I said, pretending an indifference I did not feel.

"Nonsense, we'll find out when your mom will be home. How is she?"

"Fine."

"Meaning you're all tied up in knots and can't talk about it, even to us?"

"Let her alone," Allan said quietly, picking up the cards.

"Allan, one thing you've got to learn is that you're not proposing marriage by being a friend. Shut up, April—when I first came out here I was the supreme bellyache of all time. Finally, I guess my grandmother got tired—I mean, my mom was her only daughter and she wasn't jumping for joy, either—and as she pointed out, she *was* making the meals and keeping the house clean. You can't bring them back, so you've got to go on, was what she said."

"But Mom isn't dead," I blurted out. "Oh, Doll, I'm sorry."

I jumped up to give Doll a hug, but she dove off the rock, hitting the water in a smooth shallow dive, shaking her head as she struck out. I stood watching as she swam across the creek, turned and was back in half a dozen powerful strokes. She pulled herself up, chinning the rock, and smiled.

I knew better than to apologize. I would have hated it, and Doll and I were a lot alike.

"How about the old lady tomorrow?" she asked.

Allan turned to me. "I'd like to go, how about it?"

I shrugged. What could I say? Dolly was twisting my arm, and we both knew it; but Allan wanted to go, too, so I was stuck. Maybe I could find a way to get out of it.

But I couldn't, and the next afternoon the three of us knocked on the front door of a yellow two-story frame house. It would have been an ordinary house, more newly painted than most, if it hadn't been that there was no garden, just sand with a yellow picket fence around it and a cow skull stuck up in the middle on an old piece of driftwood. Abalone shells, like those the sheriff had around his lawn, lined the yard just inside the fence, one shell leaning against each picket. The blinds on the house were all drawn, and no sound came from within. We would have thought no one lived there if we hadn't known better. There was no sign advertising fortune telling nor even a doorbell, but everyone in town knew the old woman read palms for $1.50.

Allan knocked, and the door creaked open. She must have been right behind it. At first I thought there was no one there. It was dark inside. The steel chain of a night catch gleamed in the sun. Then a woman with an incredibly lined face and the eyes of a hawk peered through the door, which did not open beyond a mere six inches. She had black hair and was dressed entirely in black, except for gold hoops at her ears.

"Yes?"

"We'd like our palms read if it's convenient, ma'am," Allan said, squeezing my hand.

"And the cards," Dolly added.

"One dollar and fifty cents apiece and one dollar extra for the cards. In advance for the palms. You can decide about the cards later." She shoved her hand, palm up, through the opening, and waited like a statue while we fished around and finally handed over the $4.50. The hand snapped shut, the longest red fingernails I'd ever seen biting into our money. The hands of a vampire.

The chain dropped, banging against the door jamb, and we entered a room so dark we could hardly see each other and only dimly perceive the chairs she indicated.

"Who is first? Step up. Step up." She spoke softly, but there was a sharp metallic command to her voice.

Dolly and I pushed Allan toward the chair by her table, but the fortune teller shook her head and pointed to me.

"I feel your vibrations," she said.

"Go ahead. She's only guessing," Allan whispered. I thought he sounded relieved that I was first.

"I bet she's sixty if she's a day—and false eyelashes," Dolly added with shaky nonchalance as she moved behind Allan.

"Shhh." The fortune teller put her bony hand on my shoulder and pushed me into the chair.

Her nails dug into my hand as they had dug into our money, and she drew it within an inch or two of her eyes. She wore rings on three fingers of each hand, and the stones sparkled, reflecting in her eyes as they stared at me out of that dark room. She sighed. Then she studied my palm for a long time, saying nothing. Whatever she saw caused her to shake her head sadly and sigh again, a long melancholy breath that left me shaking.

"Yes, yes," she said.

"Yes, what?" I could feel Allan standing behind me, kneading my shoulders.

She dropped my hand and glared at Allan and Dolly. "Sit down! Imbeciles! Interrupting the vibrations. You are destroying everything, everything." She did not take my hand again until Dolly and Allan sat in overstuffed chairs at the far side of the table.

"Ah, a good lifeline. There is a break—a long illness—at about fifty but then it tails on and on. Faint at spots, but a long life. And two marriages."

"Will I be divorced or a widow?" I asked.

"I cannot say. A great sadness. You have trouble now. I sense it, and there is a cross-hatch here in your hand. Yes, illness, but not your own. Someone in your family. Hmmm—you are afraid to make some move."

"What do you mean?" I closed my eyes and tried to pull my hand away, but she would not let go. I did not have the strength to insist. There was not a sound in the room. She was about to say something terrible, something I did not want to hear, but I could not stop it. I could not even say no. Fermine was wrong about me.

"You must stop fighting your fate," she said, fixing her hawk eyes on mine. "It will pass. It will pass. I see a smooth line ahead. A talent. You will find fulfillment in work. I see children."

"How many?" Dolly asked.

The fortune teller dropped my hand then and frowned at Dolly. "You have broken the vibration again," she said. "It is over. That is all."

"Oh, I'm sorry. I'll hush. Please."

The fortune teller sat holding her head in her hands. Was she trying to regain the vibrations? Or should I get up and give my place to Dolly or Allan. I got up.

"There is a question you wish to ask me? I feel an unanswered query in this room? Speak!" she commanded, without looking up.

"Thank you very much," I gasped.

"What do you wish to know, my dear? You must have great patience, and the solution will come—this time," she sighed again. "Maybe the cards will help," she added briskly.

"Oh, no." I didn't want to know what the cards said.

"You have had an accident. It was not important. Forget." The fortune teller stared at me with unearthly hawk eyes. I could not doubt her knowledge any more than I could move. I stood, rooted to the oriental rug before her table, even after she had waved her hands in dismissal.

"You must come again when you are ready. Enough for today. The young man next," she called.

19

DOLLY GAVE ME NO PEACE AFTER WE LEFT THE FOR-
tune teller's. She pestered me about "the accident"
until I finally broke down and told her and Allan a
little of my trip to see Mom. However, I was no
longer really afraid of the nurse since Fermine was
willing to burn down the hospital for me, so I must
have left out my horror. They were interested—
Dolly was goggle eyed—but neither of them felt I'd
been in any danger at all. They decided to go in on a
carton of cigarettes for the nasty old John whose son
had committed him. I was to take him the cigarettes
on my next visit. In fact, Allan decided to drive me
down the following Saturday. Dolly would come,
and we'd go for a picnic first.

"You don't need to worry. We won't horn in on you and your mom. We can mosey around town and come back for you," Dolly said.

"Thanks a whole lot. Suppose I just don't want to go?"

"If we start early enough, we can spend the morning on the beach first and see if it has any different species," Allan added eagerly. He was making a study of the different kinds of sea gulls inhabiting California beaches.

"But I thought you didn't want to get involved?" I truly did not want to go. This had been the happiest summer I'd ever had, so long as I did not think about visiting my mother. Still, there was a part of me that felt pretty guilty. And, I guess, I missed her, too.

"Friendship. We're not getting involved—just going along for the ride."

So the following Saturday, I was again sitting on the hospital lawn with Mom. Cigarettes, four cans of evaporated milk, and instant coffee lay between us like offerings to the gods. The sun was still shining, as if it had not gone down since my last visit. Allan had promised to return promptly at four, so he would be with me when we took her back to the waiting room. That was such a fine thing for him to do that I was almost happy.

Mom looked good. They had a swimming pool, and she was getting a tan. She was preoccupied but less nervous than the last time I'd come. Fermine had brought some prettier clothes and that helped; she looked more like herself. But, once she got over being glad to see me, there seemed little to say. Fermine had suggested I ask her if she wanted to keep the house, but I didn't know how. I was trying to remember some gossip Fermine might have missed when I realized the voice behind us was speaking to me.

"Pardon me, ma'm," he repeated softly, insistently. "But I'm looking for a girl to marry, a nice girl who'd like to travel and see the world. I ain't got much time because I'm leaving tonight, tomorrow at the latest."

I whirled around. A huge blond man, unshaven and in his early twenties, stood between me and the sun. His shadow covered me, turning the August sun dark and cold. There was a terrible pleading in his watery blue eyes, and I couldn't look away, couldn't answer him with the wisecrack that froze in my throat. He wasn't kidding. He didn't know me, it wasn't me he was looking at; he wanted his nice girl so desperately he didn't care who knew it. I shivered. My first proposal, maybe the only one I'd ever have. I looked at my mother, but she was turned away, peering across the hospital toward the mountains. Suddenly I reached down and picked up a pack of cigarettes, knowing it was no substitute, and shoved it toward him. I was careful not to look up.

"No, ma'am, that's not what I want."

"What did you say? Mom, this man's talking to

us." My mother turned, but her eyes did not focus on us.

"You see, it's this way, ma'am. I'm pulling out of this here place tonight, tomorrow at the latest, and so I'm looking for a nice girl to marry. I'd take her every place, to see the whole world and first class, too. There must be someone who'd like to travel and see the world. I'd throw in some new clothes, too, even a coat with fur on it, because if you're traveling first class and every place, you're liable to be cold sometimes. Are you ever cold?"

I shook my head, held in his stare. Served me right for wearing high heels and stockings. I had wanted to look elegant so the nurses would know I wasn't a patient, but I'd only managed to look old enough to marry. Not that he was going to choke me on the hospital lawn in the midst of a thousand Saturday visitors. He only wanted to get out of there and marry a nice girl who liked to travel. But what could *I* say to him? Would he cry if I said no? Somehow, I couldn't do that to him.

"She's only a little girl, John. This is my daughter, April. She's fourteen, not old enough for you. She has to go to high school first." My mother spoke in much the same hopeless gentle tones he used, as if she would have liked to see the wedding. The last time I'd been there she'd called the cigarette moocher John. Did she call all the men there John?

167

"Too bad," he said. "Yeah, you have such pretty hair, April. Would have been nice. I was planning to go everywhere, even Montreal. Say, you ever been to Montreal? Me neither. Say, I reckon I will take them cigs."

I was surprised that the pack was still in my hand. He thanked me as a polite stranger would and turned and shuffled slowly away. I wanted to yell after him please not to give up the trip just because I couldn't go.

"He looked as if he'd died, shriveled up because I wouldn't marry him, because I was too young," I said.

"It's so hard for the young men here," Mom said.

"Are they really letting him out tonight?"

"I doubt it." She sighed and stirred her coffee. "I was almost out of treats. Fermine thinks this is a good chance for me to stop smoking. Ah, how little he knows me."

I thought of Fermine's comment that my mother didn't know how to say no and wondered, for the first time, just what he meant, surely more than the smoking. I looked out across the lawn with its ruffle of shrubbery, the low Spanish buildings, to the bean fields and walnut grove and the mountains. I could see why Mom kept looking at those mountains; they were something to celebrate. But the sky was a monotonous blue, without a cloud or any other variation. It might as well be raining.

"A penny for your thoughts," Mom said.

"Fermine and I painted the kitchen at home. And we hauled away all the bottles in the back yard, too. Wait'll you see." I was surprised that I'd been thinking about the house, although it was generally on my mind with Susan suggesting we sublease it every time she set foot in the front door.

"So much lifting. Poor darling, but Fermine has always made neatness the prime virtue," she said, adjusting her glasses.

"He did it for you, you know. Aren't you pleased? Especially the kitchen, which was a real mess!"

Mom shrugged. "Was it? How about your dancing? Have you earned enough money for lessons?"

"Oh, I've kind of given it up." The truth was that I might need the bean money to keep our house if Susan got tough about shoving me over to Fermine's spare room. "We glued back all the chairs that were coming apart, and Fermine showed me how to wax the floors," I added eagerly.

"I'd rather see you dance than wax floors. I didn't bear my baby so she could grow up to learn to wax floors. Well, poor Fermine. I guess he can't help it, the instincts of a handyman, like my own poor mother." Mom sighed again. She muttered to herself, shaking her head violently.

"If I didn't keep our house, there wouldn't *be* all the work and then maybe I *could* take lessons. Fermine does have a spare room, you know!" The words had come rushing out because she'd put us down as if

169

she were some princess. But once they were out, I was sorry. "Oh, Mom, I didn't mean it, not really. I'll keep the house for you."

"Why? It would be less lonely, too," she said gently, as if she were comforting me. "And so good for Fermine."

"But don't you *care* if we lose our house? Where could we go when you come home?"

"There are other houses for rent, places that don't leak and have some heat. You can choose one and surprise me."

But maybe not houses where you can see the sunrise, I thought. She sounded as if it were all settled. Just like Susan. Only Fermine cared what I thought. But she was right. I *didn't* want to live in that house by myself any more. It *might* be for a long time. Maybe she and Susan thought it would be a long time before she came home. She might feel easier if I lived with Fermine.

"Ah, April, how would you like to see where *I* live, my ward?" she asked, turning to face me, smiling as if she were offering a great treat.

"Your ward? How about our house?" I exploded. Fermine was a lowly handyman for being kind enough to fix up our house so it was fit to live in, but *her* precious ward was something to behold! The first time I was there, she couldn't bear the old woman padding around all night on her "poor little feet," but the second time she wanted to show the place off.

Still, why not? Not many girls could say they were invited to tea in an insane asylum.

"I'd like them to see you," she added wistfully. "It's a different ward, nicer."

"What makes you think I like being exhibit A? It's something to do, I guess. Will they even let me in?"

"The nurse said it would be all right if you took a peek."

It was unlike Mom to plan ahead for anything. I was both curious and scared as we went down a long arched hallway, musky and damp after the hot sun outside, the dark creche shaped recesses every few hundred feet heightening the impression of a convent. Not that I'd ever been inside a convent, but I'd read about them. Being a nun seemed like voluntarily going to a prison. I used to study nun's faces, and it was a surprise to find how happy and alive most of them looked. But I had never wanted to be a nun. Nobody was going to order me around.

We stopped in front of a black door with a little glass window. Mom rang the doorbell and then stood with her nose glued against the window until some woman stared back, nodded, and a key turned smoothly.

"Mrs. Thornton said I could bring my daughter for a few minutes."

The nurse looked at me in astonishment, then shrugged and let us in.

"I'm sure it's perfectly all right with me," she said

and walked back down the corridor that opened into the ward.

"Hey, kid, are you a new admission?" a girl about my age, who was wearing a football helmet, asked.

"No, thank God, she isn't, Lottie. She's just come to visit us."

"Too bad. I thought maybe we could get up a team," Lottie said, bouncing a tennis ball. "Mary, can I have your dessert tonight?"

My mother nodded, smiled, and turned away from the girl. "Right over here is where we sleep," she said. We looked into a room as long as many of the hallways. There must have been fifty beds along each wall, facing center, each one neatly made, with a green and white striped seersucker bedspread pulled over it. Far down at the end, a patch of sunlight blazed a square on the floor and made the rest of the room seem particularly dreary. There were a few crucifixes, but otherwise nothing on the walls. There was not a picture, a photograph, a rug, a bedstand, or even a calendar in that room where my mother slept. Two women lay on their beds, staring at the ceiling. Otherwise the room was empty.

"But how do you tell which bed is yours and where do you keep your cigarettes and coffee?" I asked. It was hard to know what to say when she was standing there smiling as if it were something to be proud of.

"Best thing is to keep them in the mattress. Our names are on the beds. Want to see mine?"

"Just show me from here. But, but you can't see the sunrise—ever, can you?" I watched her face and saw a tiredness sink in. "I mean, it's sure clean and nice. Do you make your own bed?"

"It's so strange. Long ago, when I was your age, April, I wanted to be a nun, and I used to imagine the cloister as being something very much like this. Even the beds were turned to the center aisle. I used to think we would wake every morning to the pealing of church bells. We have them here on Sundays—but we've finished breakfast by the time they ring."

"I turn the bed so I see the sunrise—your bed—every morning, do you mind?"

"April, darling. I'm so glad for you," she said, hugging me. "The doctor here says I should be able to face the morning without props. Face the morning, he said. I keep thinking about the sunrise as a prop. Like putting the rainbow on a cereal box. But I suppose they work him too hard around here for him to enjoy sunrises, poor man."

The girl in the football helmet was waiting when we reached what Mom called the day room. There were plenty of windows there, but the flowered curtains were drawn because most of the women were watching a slide show. A travelogue of mountains somewhere. A few watched the fish in two aquariums, and a few more were playing cards and checkers. Everyone turned and stared at us, their eyes glassy, fish eyes. Tranquilizers, I thought.

"There she is. Didn't I tell you Mary brought her daughter?" football helmet shouted triumphantly.

"Such a pretty girl."

"You done right well, Mary."

"You come to take your mother out of this hellhole?" one old lady asked. She was almost bald, and her hand kept smoothing what hair she had over her ears. Her voice sounded just like the voice of the old man who'd asked me the same thing the first time I visited the hospital.

"You got a quarter so I can make a phone call?" the football helmet girl asked.

"Not unless she had a quarter for each of us," the old woman growled. So I shook my head at the girl.

"You shut up, you old witch," Lottie in the helmet yelled.

"Who are you calling names?"

The atmosphere became tense without warning, and I felt something closing in on me. I didn't want to get caught in a fight. Suddenly the room was silent. Everyone stopped talking. The nurse had stopped the slide show.

"She'll start again when everyone's quiet. Don't worry," my mother said, pulling me quickly out of the day room and back down the hall. Another nurse let us out, and I breathed deeply.

I could see the young girl peering through the little window.

"She is such a creep," I said, though that wasn't exactly what I meant. "Why did you give her your dessert?"

"When Lottie first came, she smashed her guitar on that door and now she cries for it in the night, poor girl. It's hard to sleep, and so the other women get angry."

"Is there a lot of fighting?" The words slipped out. I'd promised myself all the way down not to ask how things were. We both knew they were lousy, but there wasn't much either of us could do.

"We help each other most of the time. It's hard for everyone, and most of the women help if they can." She was looking at me intensely in the way near-sighted people do when there is something important to say. I could see that she wasn't bothering to pull out the grey hairs anymore. She took my hand and held it to her cheek.

"How is your friend, Allan?" Mom asked, finally. I knew that that wasn't what she wanted to say. Maybe next time I came she'd say more. At the very least, next time I could ask about the bald lady and the girl in the football helmet.

"He'll be here in a few minutes to drive me home," I answered, and felt time closing in on us again, as if Allan were already walking down the hall. I felt my mother's hand tremble against my cheek, and I knew that if I looked up I would see fear in her eyes. We hadn't settled what I should do about our house, and I knew she wanted a promise about when I would come again. I lay my head on her shoulder, but I could say nothing.

"What do you want—about the house?" Mom asked.

"I want to live with Fermine, I guess." Somehow the words seemed harsh, perhaps because I'd said live instead of stay. It sounded so permanent. My mother held me at arm's length. Her eyes were gentle.

"Don't worry," she said. "Don't worry. Sooner or later we all have to learn to celebrate the morning without props."

Her tone was reassuring, the same voice she'd used so many months before, after Susan got upset about the gas incident, when she said I was her daughter and no one could take me away. I wondered if that could be true, even now. I wanted to ask, but she was staring off into space, looking down the hall as if she, too, were waiting. I knew that my visit was over.

"All the same, you like sweets so much you shouldn't be giving away your desserts," I said, trying to bring her back.

But there was no answer.

We leaned against the cool plaster wall in the semi-darkness of the empty hall until I heard footsteps; far down the hall, Dolly and Allan were coming toward us, their steps loud in our separate silences.

"I'll bring sugar for your coffee when I come next time," I said, waving at my friends. Then I knocked on her ward door, and I saw football helmet run for the nurse. She should unlock the door just about the time Dolly and Allan reached us. Gently, I took my mother's hand from my cheek and held it between my own, waiting.